Wildball

BRIAN ENGLES

Black Rose Writing | Texas

8/22

ISBN: 978-1-68433-032-4
PUBLISHED BY BLACK ROSE WRITING
www.blackrosewriting.com

Printed in the United States of America
Suggested Retail Price (SRP) $17.95

Wildball is printed in Palatino Linotype

FOR THOMAS, MASON, AND RORY.

Praise for *Wildball*

"*Wildball* evokes what W.P. Kinsella called 'the thrill of the grass,' as we spend a seaside summer in lower-level ball, with Shane, a young player caught in the rundown of mixed emotions about a man who was both mentor and tormentor. It's a novel sure to enthrall fans of the game and those who enjoy stories of rich and complex relationships."

William McKeen, author of *Outlaw Journalist*

"More than just a sports themed book... Engles moves a gutsy pen by bringing an extremely difficult subject to light through the eyes of an up-and-coming college baseball player. Shane Monaghan's tumultuous yet inspiring season playing summer ball will be an especially important read for any young man who is struggling to find the courage to reveal his own secret. This book will help him take that step."

T.M. Murphy, co-author of *The Running Waves*

"Any baseball fan will love this book! A bit of nostalgia for anyone familiar with the Cape Cod Baseball League. Engles effectively captures the mind of a baseball player overcoming a troubled past."

Dr. Lani Lawrence, Doctor of Sports Psychology

"In *Wildball*, Engles crafts a captivating and wildly entertaining narrative about come to terms with and confronting the toxic masculinity that is so pervasive in society - and especially in sports. It is compulsively readable and highly recommended."

Dylan Fernandes, Massachusetts State Representative

Wildball

CHAPTER ONE

"Lost Boys"

Growing up out West, Shane witnessed a handful of forest fires, but never one that emitted such a menacing glow. He examined the night sky from the ballpark and the thick wisps of crimson fog that hovered in the distance. It was a violent shade of red, like some kind of Northern Lights gone wrong. He half expected the ominous cloud to build and descend onto Hinton Fields, consuming the Brigs in one gulp. But the fog remained in place, floating and stagnant.

"Shane! What's taking you so long?" Coach Hale called from the diamond.

He turned back to his team. They all seemed puzzled by his prolonged trip to left field. "Do you guys see...?" Shane trailed off, realizing the only thing his new teammates were staring at was him. If it was a sign of inferno, Shane thought, then there would have been sirens and these guys would have tossed their gloves down in panic. He scanned the field for the grounder that slipped past him when the hellish smoke claimed his focus.

Shane whipped the ball back towards home and jogged to his place in the middle infield, trying to force the devil sky out of his mind. Max DeMello stood before him, looking nonchalant as he checked his watch.

"You okay, Shane?"

Somehow Max already knew everyone's names on the first night of practice.

Did he make flashcards on the plane ride here? I should've done that.

Shane readied for the alternating grounders he and Max were taking rapid-fire as Max hustled over to his side. "What's the hold up?" Shane asked.

"Your face, bro." Max pointed at his nose.

He thought it was just sweat, as he wiped his upper lip he saw blood covering his fingers. "Aw, shit."

"Does he have a nosebleed?" the catcher shouted from home plate.

"Yeah. Anybody have a towel?" Max asked.

Shane clamped down on the bridge of his nose. He took off his shirt and used it to stem the flow of blood. In the corner of his eye, he spotted the red fog creeping into sight. He shut his eyes and stood still.

"Don't tilt your head like that," Max advised. "The blood will go down your throat."

"I get these sometimes," Shane explained. "I just need some ice on the back of my neck and it'll slow everything down."

"Let's call it a night, gents," Coach Hale shouted. "We've got a first aid kit in the locker room."

"Looks like you're shortstop," Shane said to Max.

"You did fine." Max patted him on the shoulder and guided him towards the Burnsdale Recreation Center.

Shane heard the clanging of baseballs falling into a milk crate as the rest of the boys cleaned up the field. He opened his eyes again once they arrived at the Rec, but lingered on the dirt track that surrounded the field.

"You coming?" Max asked.

"One second," Shane said, eying the skyline. Off the field it was clear that red lights from distant metal towers had illuminated the hovering fog, tricking Shane into a state of panic. He glanced up to make sure the red fog wouldn't follow him inside, that it wasn't about to swallow up the coastal town on this apocalyptic evening of early June.

• • •

Shane sat in the brown folding chair across from Hale's desk, unconcerned about Coach calling him in to chat.

"I have some tissues here in case your nose acts up again," Hale said. His name was embroidered on the left breast of his maroon polo, which was a little snug on him and pronounced the girth of his belly.

"Thanks, Coach. I'm good now."

Hale's office, a cramped closet in the far corner of the Rec Center, overlooked the Burnsdale Brigs' home turf of Hinton Fields from a small window next to his desk. There were photos of previous teams hanging on the walls, with Coach wearing the same proud smile in each shot. Fluorescent bulbs released a greenish light that pooled in the room, highlighting stacks of manila folders full of player stats and medical records.

"What'd you want to talk about?" Shane asked.

"I was looking in your file earlier and I realized I still didn't have a letter of recommendation from someone at your high school."

"But my coach at GSU said –"

"Don't worry. You're all set to be here. I just like to get the whole picture of who our guys are." Coach dialed back the volume of the country music on his radio. "So I called up St. Francis... and I got some troubling news."

Shane's fingers perspired as he gripped the bottom of his chair.

"I know we're just meeting tonight, but you're my player now," Hale said. "I want you to hear this from me instead of finding out online."

"What's going on?" Shane felt his ears turn red. He hated how his physical response to anxiety was such an obvious tell. "Did you talk to Coach Calloway? Did he say something about me?"

"I'm guessing no one from home has called you?"

"My phone was off for practice."

Hale flipped through Shane's file as if a guide to breaking bad news might magically appear between the pages. On top of the papers was Shane's grinning player photo from Goslyn State University. Hale kept his eyes on the picture as he spoke: "I'm sorry to be the one to tell you this, but Coach Calloway is dead."

"Wait...What?" Shane's pulse overwhelmed him, beating in his chest and fingers and ears.

Hale searched through Shane's file. He made it halfway through before he closed the folder. "I spoke to him briefly in the winter and I thought I could find my notes."

"When did he die?"

"It just happened today."

"How?"

"In a car wreck... The assistant coach I talked to at St. Francis said he crashed into a tree... No one's called you?"

"No one called." Shane took off his hat and rubbed his temple. He tuned into the static coming through the radio and stared at the floor until the tiles blurred.

"Can I go?" Shane stood from his chair, eager to escape.

"Of course. I'm here if you need to talk."

"Thanks, Coach. I think I'd rather work it out on the field."

•   •   •

Shane craned his neck, but the floodlights hindered any chance of stargazing. His eyes drifted back to the vacant baseball diamond and grassy terrain of Hinton Fields.

He considered calling his mom to talk about Calloway, but he kept his phone off to avoid the flood of texts from St. Francis kids he hadn't spoken to in months. Shane heard footsteps behind him and worried they might belong to Coach Hale on his way out of the Rec. When he turned back, he saw a group of adolescent boys entering the nearby basketball court.

Metallic pings rang out as Shane went down the bleachers. He walked across the field and crawled through the broken corner in the chain-link fence where kids snuck into the games even though there was no admission fee.

Still restless and ill, he was not ready to return to his host family's house. He dashed across the street before he could be illuminated by an oncoming vehicle's headlights, cleared the wooden guardrail, and made a clean landing in the brush. Behind the ballpark was a vast pond Shane had yet to explore.

The trails around the pond were overgrown and hard to navigate, but the squish of mud under his feet signaled he was getting closer to the water. Shane hunched down and clawed at the grass with his fingers.

"What happened to Calloway?" he asked aloud. "Was he drunk? Was he texting? Did he go flying? Was it quick?"

Unsurprisingly, the pond didn't have any answers about his former coach's fate, but when he peered upward Shane saw a bright red dot in the sky from the same wicked towers that tricked him at infielders practice.

"What am I even doing here?"

"Don't make me go back there!" a voice responded. It was half-shout, half-mumble, and terrified.

Shane jumped up, startled.

Who was that?

He held his breath and could make out muffled snoring. Shane began to sneak his way around the edge of the pond to investigate.

The volume of his steps seemed thunderous as he went through thick vines and fallen branches, snapping underfoot. Then he felt resistance against his shoe before it hit the grass; beneath him was a small person. Shane pulled back and squinted, waiting for his eyes to adjust to the darkness.

In front of him was a boy sleeping on his side, maybe twelve years of age, whose fragmented snoring no longer seemed panicked. His hands were pressed together, forming a pillow for his head. Black hair framed a seemingly calm freckled face, off-set by a swelling bruise on his cheekbone, still fresh and not yet purple. Shane worried if he abandoned the boy some creep might show up later and discover him in this vulnerable state.

"Hey. Get up," Shane said, shaking the kid's shoulder.

The boy woke up quick. He scrambled into consciousness and clawed an object out of the dirt.

Shane watched as the kid leapt up and settled into a crooked fighting pose, keeping his left fist close for defense and clutching a pocketknife in his right.

"It's okay. I'm not gonna hurt you," Shane said.

The boy brushed his black hair out of his face to get a better look at the stranger before him. It was then he noticed the blade of his knife was still folded close in its case. He unsheathed the small weapon and held his stance.

"Easy...." Shane placed his arms up in surrender. "My name's Shane. I play for the Brigs, right across the street. What are you doing out here?"

"I... I think I fell asleep," the boy said then squinted his eyes. He commenced some kind of unannounced staring contest with Shane and concluded he was not a threat. The boy relaxed his shoulders and put the knife in his back pocket. "Careful," he warned. "You're about to step in that poison ivy."

"Huh?" Shane saw a patch of the glossy plant at his feet. "Thanks."

"I gotta go."

"Don't you have a mom? Someone I can call to come pick you up?"

The boy ignored the question and darted out of the woods.

Shane checked the spot where the kid had slept and saw there was a necklace on the ground. "Hey, you forgot this."

The boy was out of earshot, so Shane took the chain in his hands and grasped the crucifix pendant attached to it.

He felt initials etched into the wood. "L.N.K," he read aloud. "Who are you?"

Shane looked up to the black sky then placed the necklace in his pocket.

CHAPTER TWO

"Wait the Wrath"

The Brigs warmed up on the diamond, except for Shane, who was safe in the shade beneath the bleachers. His eyelids were heavy, but he fought off sleep; he would be batting seventh and playing centerfield in ninety minutes time.

Coach Hale lowered himself onto the bleachers as Shane climbed up through the metal seating and sat beside him. "You have a minute?" Shane said.

Hale jumped, tossing a handful of trail mix he was about to enjoy. "Holy Jesus!" Hale yelled as raisins and nuts rained down on him. "Shane, where in the hell you pop up from?"

"Sorry. Didn't mean to scare you."

"Well, you did." Hale wiped crumbs off his windbreaker. "You ready for the game?"

"I saw I'm at center again. You think you'll use me at shortstop at all this summer?"

"I want you to focus on offense right now."

Shane had yet to make a hit during the first week of Cove League play. "I feel like this could be a big night for me."

"Know a better way to start off a big night?" Hale spat a raisin towards the field. "Warm up with your teammates. Don't nap under the bleachers."

•   •   •

The sky was still bright and blue at six o'clock as Shane and Lucas stretched their legs on the grass. On the far side of the field, the Waterford Breakers geared up for the game.

Lucas Barnes was the towering leftfielder for the Brigs. His long hair was the same color as hardwood oak and his Southern accent reminded Shane of the Westerns he used to watch as a kid. Lucas grinned at the sight of a short eleven-year-old boy jogging towards the dugout with bats for the Brigs.

"Gus," Lucas called.

The two tapped fists after the boy approached, the first step in an elaborate secret handshake. They extended their fingers, used their hands to gesture like big waves coursing through the sea, and finished with something similar to a thumb war before Gus resumed his trek to the dugout.

"We came up with that in workshops last year." It was Lucas' second summer in the Cove League. At twenty-two, Lucas was Burnsdale's oldest player while Shane was the youngest at nineteen.

Lexi Henson, the Brigs' field reporter and daughter of Shane's host family, sauntered across the park to shortstop Max DeMello. Lexi leaned down and pushed Max's knee closer to his torso as he reclined in the grass, stretching his hips and back.

"You think those two are hooking up?" Shane asked.

"I don't know," Lucas said. "Why? Are you jealous of Mighty Max?"

"No."

"Well, I am. He already has the best bat. And he's pretty dope at short."

"Fine. I'm jealous." Shane stood up and swatted grass clippings off his red pinstriped pants. "And I'm pissed these uniforms make me look like a giant candy cane."

"Hey, before you head out, I wanted to ask you..." Lucas tightened his cleats then got up from the ground. "My church is having this big event for kids on Sunday and we need volunteers to help out."

"Don't we have a game that day?"

"Nope. It's an off-day."

"I don't know, Lucas. That's not really my thing."

"What? Volunteering?"

"No, church."

Shane walked away from the starters doing their warm-ups while families trickled into the park, filling in the last open spots on Spectator's Hill. A copy of the night's program tumbled by on the dirt, so Shane bent down and snatched it. The rosters for both teams along with each player's stats were listed on the front. There was a blurb on the back about how the Cove League was the premiere collegiate association for summer ball, where the country's best athletes competed in this pipeline to the Majors.

He handed the program over to a confused camera operator for the local TV station. Discarded peanut shells and pieces of goose shit gathered under Shane's cleats on his way to the dugout. A pack of kids in line by the concessions shack grew quiet as he drew near. He tipped his cap and smiled as they broke out into a frenzy of whispers. Seasoned fans huddled up discussing which players from last summer's batch were selected in the draft. The radio announcers tested their microphones at a rectangular table while the field interns set up tents to provide shade.

Shane was starting to feel the charge. He always liked the previews better than the movie, and sometimes the minutes building up to a game could be filled with more promise than the following nine innings could ever deliver.

•   •   •

It was still scoreless as dusk crept over the fifth inning. The Brigs were up to bat with two outs against them. After a single from Max, the home team fans looked to Shane to keep the momentum going.

The Waterford pitcher's name was Andy Bergan and he was dominating the mound. Shane had felt claustrophobic during the first at-bat with Andy's inside fastballs coming closer each time. He managed to make contact once, but the hit made for an easy ground out. A chance at redemption presented itself in the fifth, as Shane received a bat from Gus and watched Max take a broad step off first base.

"Up next for the Burnsdale Brigs, all the way from Goslyn State in Oregon, give it up for Shane Monoghan," the P.A. announcer said.

The distorted bass and thick drums of "Crawl" by Kings of Leon blasted over the speakers. The song amped him up for his short march to the plate then it quickly faded away. In the quiet that followed, Shane found his grip and waited while the pitcher and catcher settled on their first move.

Bergan elevated his left leg, bent it at the knee, and drew his glove close to his chest. His leg came forward and he launched a fastball to Shane.

The crack of the wooden bat was still new to him; sharper and more severe than the familiar clunk of the metal he was used to back in Oregon. Once he finished processing the foreign sound, Shane sprinted for first, letting his bat drop to the dirt.

The Waterford outfielders raced for the rolling ball, but Shane and Max both advanced safely before a play could be made.

"Go Brigs! Go Brigs!" the fans chanted.

Shane hid his exhilaration, wanting to seem poised in front of Max, who directed a head nod of approval his way. As Shane caught his breath, the Brigs' first base coach rewarded his inaugural Cove League hit with a friendly pat on the butt.

Roman DeGrazio, the brawny third baseman, stepped up to the plate next. He spotted his elderly host parents in the crowd before he brought the bat to his shoulders. Don and Dorothy Miller waved at Roman. They attended each home game and littered the field with butterscotch candy wrappers while they watched. Roman had passed up socializing with his teammates over the first week in order to get to know his host parents. Each night they listened to vinyl records while the couple shared stories from their sixty years of marriage.

The charge was palpable. The molecules in the air changed like a dizzying contagion spreading among them: Max, Shane, Roman, the boys in the dugout, Coach Hale, Gus, they could all sense something was about to boil over.

After a ball and a strike, Roman knocked a fastball into left field and the three Brigs ran. Max had taken a healthy lead and was already rounding third. Shane followed behind, glanced to the right, and realized the outfielders were about to recover the ball.

The third base coach held his open palms to Shane, signifying him to hit the brakes. Then a roar came from the crowd as Max reached home.

I want it more.

Shane ignored his instructions and made a dash for it. He watched the catcher come forth with his glove open, hungry for the out. With the ball closing in behind him, Shane fell into a slide. His right leg burned from friction and his opponent's body on top of him. The strange mix of adrenaline and inertia made him lightheaded. His left hand smeared the dust on home plate. He turned to the umpire, waiting for the call.

The man stuck both his arms out flat, declaring Shane safe as the crowd went wild.

●   ●   ●

A few kids played catch under the floodlights, but most of the fans had left Hinton Fields for the night. Shane was on the warning track, loading gear into the broadcast van when Lexi approached with a microphone in hand.

"You want an interview?" she asked.

He followed her to right field where her camera was already mounted on a tripod. "Heads up," Lexi said. "I might ask you a personal question."

"Okay... Wait. Can I check my hair first?"

"Just keep your hat on." Lexi hit record and walked back into frame.

Shane tucked his thumbs under his belt loops and rested his hands on his side.

"We're rolling." She cleared her throat and brought the microphone to her face. "Good evening. I'm Lexi Henson with the Brigs Blog and I'm talking to Shane Monoghan, centerfielder for the team.

"Shane, after a slow start, you were integral in the win over the Breakers tonight. Tell me, what changed so that you were able to start contributing offensively?"

"I always circle the runway before I land," he said. "Luckily Coach Hale was patient while I got comfortable."

"I imagine part of the adjustment process has been playing centerfield instead of shortstop. What have you done to acclimate to the outfield?"

"The angles are the biggest thing," Shane said. "I'm used to reading pitches from the infield, but with center it's different. You're trying to track the ball's movement from a new spot. Then these things like how you position your body, or how much ground you have to cover, all this stuff that used to be second nature, is suddenly a challenge again."

"I know you're going through a difficult time right now. Last week you lost your high school coach, Mike Calloway. How has that affected your Cove League experience?"

Shane's gaze wandered to the departing families. He saw a little girl with ketchup and mustard stains on her face and an oversized Brigs cap on her head. He stared at the kid as if somehow she could save him from Lexi's ambush. "I'm sorry. What?"

"Has your coach's death affected your experience here?" Lexi asked.

"Uh, it was a definitely shock. I've just been trying... just been trying to do my best."

"What part did Coach Calloway have in your development as a player?"

"Um… He always wanted me to leave it all on the field. Taught me to push myself further than I thought I could go."

"Were there any specific lessons you want to share?"

She's not dropping this.

Shane rubbed his chin with his thumb and index finger.

Stop doing that. You don't even have facial hair.

The warm sensation in his ears kicked in. "He always wanted me to do my homework. Study different pitches…I'm not sure."

"It must be bittersweet to have success like this," Lexi said. "Playing in such a celebrated league, when you've lost your mentor. Has it had an impact on your performance here?"

He swallowed his spit and squinted, fighting to keep his eyes dry. He focused on the grass under his cleats.

What did she say?

"I always try to clear my head before a game and … Even though what happened, even though Coach, Mr. Calloway is, since he passed – What it comes down to is that you have to put those things out of your mind when you're on the field."

"Glad we got to talk, Shane. Thanks for your time."

Lexi waited for Shane to thank her back, but instead an awkward silence followed. She went behind the camera and turned off her equipment.

"How did you know about Calloway?" Shane asked.

Before Lexi could answer, she was swooped up in Max's light brown arms. He held Lexi in the air for a moment before setting her back down. "Are you finished?"

"Way to keep it professional." Lexi brushed dust off her blazer.

"How was your interview?" Max asked Shane.

"It was great." Shane pushed the tripod over and it fell to the ground with a thud. He went towards the Rec before Lexi could react.

"What the hell?" she shouted after a moment.

"Hold up." Max caught up with Shane and pulled him down into the dugout. "Why'd you get so heated?"

"She was asking me about…"

"Asking you about what?" Max asked.

You can't talk to him about Calloway.

"She was asking about how I got moved to the outfield," Shane said.

"You're still mad you're not playing short?" Max took off his Brigs cap and clasped its bill in his hands. "That's a dumb reason for us to not be friends."

"I know," Shane said, surprised avoiding one conflict had led to settling another. "I'm sorry."

"You might want to apologize to Lexi instead," Max said. "Or just go into hiding."

"But you and me are cool?"

"Of course." Max wrapped Shane up in a big hug. "We just have to be honest with each other. Okay?"

"Okay." Shane tried to embrace, but his body felt constricted.

The floodlights cut, leaving the ballpark dark and lonely as Max released Shane from his arms.

CHAPTER THREE

"Death Wish"

Shane stood naked in the Henson's bathroom and checked his reflection in the mirror. The humidity was causing his brown bangs to curl and fall disheveled across his forehead. He looked at his pointed nose and his hazel eyes before a clanking sound knocked him out of his trance. Just as he realized he had forgotten his clean towel back in his room, the ancient door handle turned and Lexi walked inside.

"Whoa!" Shane covered his crotch.

"I'm sorry." Lexi rushed backward and closed the door.

"It's alright. I'm finished anyway." He threw on his briefs and braved the hallway.

"I'm sorry," Lexi said again.

"My bad. I thought I had it locked."

"It's not a big deal. I've seen worse."

Shane gazed down at his groin.

"No. Sorry I didn't mean it like that. I just meant –"

"I gotcha." Shane caught a whiff of her mango conditioner when he passed. The scent redeemed having to clean her black hairs out of the shower drain in the mornings. "Well... I'm going to put pants on now."

"You do that." Lexi closed the bathroom door.

The Hensons lived in Devil's Foot, a village in the south of Burnsdale. It used to be a hub for commercial fishing but had become a pit stop for tourists vacationing on Eleanor's Island.

Shane slept in a spare room on the second floor of the Henson house. From one window, he could see Fred's junkyard. Bicycle tires, car parts, and toolboxes were scattered across wooden planks and out-of-commission automobiles. Shane was unsure if Mr. Henson enjoyed bringing his work as an engineer home with him or if he was trying to build a DeLorean-like time travel device in the front yard.

The second window in Shane's room looked over Marie's garden. Sometimes in the evenings he spotted her watering lace-cap hydrangeas or cutting back the English Ivy that crawled up the stone wall behind the house.

Shane ran his belt through the last loop of his jeans and heard a knock on the door. "Come in."

Fred entered the room. "I overheard what happened. You'll have to forgive Lexi. She's used to being an only child."

"It's no big deal. I just wish it hadn't been a cold shower." Shane slipped into a lightweight Brigs hoodie and hung his towel over the door.

"While you were in there a woman named Robin Calloway called for you on our house phone."

Shane felt a lump form in his throat. "What did she say?"

How did she even know how to reach me here?

"Not much," Fred said. "She left her number and asked you to call her back. Her voice was very attractive."

"It's not like that."

"Mysterious phone calls from an older woman... Flashing my daughter in the bathroom. What kind of scoundrel did the Cove League send me?"

"Might not be too late to exchange me for a different kid."

"Dinner will be ready in a few." Fred patted him on the shoulder with a rust-covered hand and left the room.

"Need me to set the table?" Shane asked.

"You set it for lefties."

"I *am* a lefty."

•   •   •

His first helpings of tuna steak, salad, and rice pilaf were almost gone.

"Don't inhale your food," Mom would say.

Take a breath. Count your chews.

He placed his silverware on his plate and eyed the Hensons.

They're all so lanky. Is there some competitive family basketball league they can join?

He saw Lexi got her dark hair from her half-Japanese father and her freckles and fair-skinned complexion from her white mother.

"So Shane, how did your interview with Lexi go?" Marie asked.

"It was..." He blanked, pushing food around his plate instead of answering.

"Uh oh," Fred said. "What happened? Lexi, were you mean to Shane?"

"No, Dad. Thanks for making that assumption though." She stopped cutting fish to point a vengeful knife at her father. "Mom, when do you break ground on the new garden?"

"Tomorrow. At the Town Green."

"You have a big project starting up?" Shane asked.

"Marie was selected by the Burnsdale Garden Club to design something for the summer fair," Fred said.

"I'm calling it a Peace Garden," Marie clarified.

"And we're very proud."

"Oh, so now that *the town* has acknowledged my work you're proud?"

"It's a big deal because Burnsdale always picks these real kitschy, seashell kinda landscape designers," Lexi explained to Shane. "But this year they picked Mom and the space is right in the center of the Town Green, so I think she should make a statement with it."

"Come on, I don't want to bore Shane with all this," Marie said.

"I can talk about things besides baseball," he said.

"Oh, that isn't what I meant. I wasn't sure how much interest you had in hearing about the garden. That's all."

"I'm interested. So by calling it a Peace Garden is it supposed to be a statement against war?"

"For me it's more about creating a space where people can feel safe. Lexi might be playing up the political angle."

Shane placed a napkin over the remnants of his dinner. "A friend of mine back in Oregon is in the army."

"That's surprising to hear about a young person making that choice right now."

Shane drank water but it went down the wrong pipe. "What's so bad about enlisting?" He asked after his coughing fit.

"I don't know if people ever really recover from war. And I don't know why someone would go out of their way to experience that trauma," Marie said.

"To keep other people safe... So they can play in their gardens," he mumbled.

"What was that?"

"Nothing."

The floor squeaked as Shane pushed his chair out. "Thanks for dinner, Mrs. Henson. It was great."

The family watched as he cleared his place and retreated upstairs.

"You can call me Marie."

●　　　●　　　●

Re: Calloway June 18
Jenny Monoghan

Hi Shane,

I went to Coach Calloway's wake yesterday. He saw so much potential in you. But he could be so harsh on you too. I remember your sophomore year when you would come home crying. I wanted to get him fired. I sent emails to your school I never told you about. I don't know what to make of his death, so I can only imagine what you're going through.

I saw Mrs. Calloway at the wake and she was asking for you. I know you don't like me giving out your cell, so I told her to contact the Cove League to get your host family's info.

Things in Astors are the same. I've been busy with work, but it's harder to be on my feet all day, starting to feel older. Your brother didn't get that post office job. Will you give him a call? You have to be the first to reach out with Troy. You're both so stubborn.

I want to hear about your season so give me a call when you can. I'm here if you need to talk about Calloway.

Love,
Mom

The note spurred him to search for new articles about Calloway and he found an expansive report from an Astors paper that was just published. He skimmed the piece; well-attended funeral, quote from saddened family members, uncertainties about cause of crash, phone records indicating Calloway was not using a device at the time, success with the St. Francis baseball program and participation in local adult hockey league, loved ones left behind.

In between two of the paragraphs was a picture of Shane and Calloway at last year's State Champs, each of them with an arm slung around the other's back and forced grins on their faces. Calloway was his usual goliath self, but Shane was shocked by how scrawny he seemed compared to his muscular coach.

Do something else.

The game tomorrow against Northam. Research the pitcher.

Hale told him to look up a kid named Palemento from the Midwest. Shane found a few game clips on YouTube of his mean curveball and noticed how Palemento saved it for his out pitch. Just as Shane's eyes began to ache, Lucas poked his head in the room.

"Ever heard of knocking?" Shane asked.

"Sorry. Were you jacking off?" Lucas swung the door open and came into the bedroom.

"Checking out Palemento."

"I don't know her videos."

"He's the Terns pitcher," Shane said, still not amused. "I'm trying to prep for tomorrow."

"Gotcha. So you're not too busy to hang out then?"

"I don't know, Lucas. I'm beat."

"But I already drove over here."

Shane groaned and shut his laptop. "I don't remember asking you to."

"Jeesh. Who spat in your oatmeal?"

"That's not an expression." Shane got off the chair and grabbed his Brigs hat. When he picked up the cap, he revealed the crucifix necklace underneath.

Lucas stared at the wooden cross. "Where'd you get that?" He lifted the necklace from the desk.

"It's some kid's. I didn't get his name," Shane said. "He left it at the pond by Hinton –"

"What kid? When did you see him?"

"It was like two weeks ago now. First night we got here. The kid was sleeping in the woods. I woke him up and then –"

"Did it look like he was in middle school? Lots of freckles?"

"That sounds right. Do you know him?"

"It had to be Noah." Lucas pointed to the initials carved into the wood: L.N.K.

"Who is he?"

"Noah Kinton. He was in the youth workshops last summer. I remember that necklace because we swapped for a day, just as a random joke. He made a big deal about how his was monogrammed and mine wasn't." Lucas pulled his own gold cross necklace out from underneath his shirt. "Then halfway through the summer the kid vanished. Never came to workshops again."

"Why'd he stop coming?"

"No idea. I didn't mean to freak you out. I just was not expecting you to have this." Lucas returned the necklace.

"Do you think he'll come to the youth workshops this summer?"

"Who knows?" Lucas said. "Maybe he'll come looking for that cross."

•   •   •

They rode around Burnsdale in the '94 Corolla Lucas drove up all the way from Louisiana. The CD player was busted, the windshield seemed to be coated in condensation no matter the weather, and the floor was littered with brown paper bags from fast food joints.

Shane took a good look at Lucas, absorbed in his task of helming the steering wheel. His dirty blonde hair almost touched his shoulders.

"You gonna grow those locks out all summer?" Shane asked.

"We'll see how the local ladies take to 'em." Lucas tucked his hair behind his ears then turned the car onto a winding back road. They hunted Burnsdale for little green dudes: plastic figures that looked like small men and had the word SLOW written across their bodies. They were a neon shade of green and held onto attached red flags. Lucas used to collect little green dudes with buddies back in his hometown and with Shane's help he had already lifted two for his Cove League collection.

Shane scanned the airwaves for anything besides commercials, static, or soft rock. He heard an impassioned sermon on a religious station.

"Hey, man. I'm sorry about blowing off that church thing last week." Shane switched off the radio. "Faith's never been a big part of my life."

"Don't sweat it. If you ever want to come to a service with my host family sometime –"

"I don't know, Luke. Ask me next Sunday."

Lucas maintained the Corolla's fast speed around a curve, causing a clamor in the back. "Shit. Are the kids okay?"

Shane saw the green dudes were flipped upside down. "'Fraid not."

"Sorry 'bout that turn, boys," Lucas shouted to the backseat. "Now, where did y'all say the hot girls hang out 'round here?"

•   •   •

They arranged the little green dudes in a clearing by the pond. Lucas found a sign posted from one of the local research facilities that put the water quality at a 'Fair' level, with a score of 37 out of 100.

"This swamp is only two points away from being 'Poor,'" Lucas noted.

"It's not a swamp. Look out for poison ivy though." Shane approached the edge of the water and knelt before it.

Lucas stood behind him, adjusting the green dudes so they were symmetrical. "That night you found Noah, why were you out here?"

"I don't want to throw a bunch of negative shit your way."

"Throw me yours, I'll throw you some of mine." Lucas sat cross-legged on the dirt. "I rigged it so I could come back to the Cove League. I withdrew from one of my classes last semester so my graduation would be delayed."

"Why would you do that?"

"If I had finished on time I wouldn't have been eligible to compete this summer," Lucas said. "I was overlooked in the draft, so I'm hoping with all the scouts that come through here I'll catch a lucky break."

"Someone will find you."

"Thanks, man. Guess it's your turn now."

Shane kept his back to Lucas as he spoke: "My coach from high school, he died right around the same time the season started out here. And I haven't been sleeping well since."

"I'm sorry. Were you two close?"

"I don't know if there's a word for what we were."

"What do you mean?"

Shane stood up and paced along the water. "Lexi is already asking questions about it. How long 'til someone else picks up the trail? All this shit is gonna come out. I mean… the guy's wife is calling my host family's house."

"Did you talk to her?"

"I can't. You don't get it. Coach Calloway, that was his name, I hated him."

"Why?"

"I don't even know what I'm doing here, man. I just didn't want to be home this summer." Shane's voice quivered. "Could you imagine? Bumping into him at the grocery store?"

"What happened with you two?"

"Senior year... I wanted him to die. I used to wish for it. Then, my first night here he gets in a car wreck... And there was this red sky. And I could feel him up there..." Shane grabbed his stomach. "Hanging over me... like I brought him out here with me."

His sternum felt like it was going to crack as a poison inside coursed through his torso. He dropped to his knees and puked by the pond.

Lucas patted Shane on the back. "Well, buddy. I think you just bumped this watering hole down from Fair to Poor."

"Good one," Shane said, the burn of stomach acid strong in his mouth.

"What the hell did this guy do to you?"

CHAPTER FOUR

"No Kin"

He tasted sunscreen and sweat on his lips as he peered up at the cloudless sky over Hinton Fields.

Noah Kinton stood before him, wielding an aluminum bat like it was a longsword. "Should my feet be out further?" he asked.

"Yes." Shane watched as the boy stretched his legs to an impractical length. "But don't do a split."

Noah drew his feet back in. His stance during scrimmage earlier in the day was rigid and awkward, so Noah's coach sent him to the batting cages for the afternoon.

"You're real tense up-top," Shane said.

"I should ease up?" Noah's voice was still tender for thirteen. He was thin and shorter than the other eighth graders in the workshop.

"Put the bat down for a sec. Take a big breath and when you exhale shake out your arms, you're too hunched up in your shoulders. This need to be more relaxed." He tapped the base of the boy's neck and Noah recoiled.

"Whoa – Sorry," Shane said, giving Noah more space. "Try it on your own. See if it helps."

"Okay." After a few shallow breaths Noah inhaled deeply, closed his eyes and flailed his arms by his side. His shoulders sank as the air came out.

Shane thought about the kid's jumpiness and his shiner at the pond. But the sea of freckles on his face was clear; the bruise had faded over the weeks. Shane hadn't mentioned the encounter yet. He feared talking about it might be embarrassing and he wasn't sure if Noah would even recognize him as the stranger that woke him that night.

"What are they doing over there?" Noah broke his stance and pointed across the field.

Lucas led the other kids through an obstacle course in left field. Beyond them, Shane could see Lexi on the warning track, her camera pointed at Max as he performed push-ups on the ground.

"Maybe they're making one of those montage scenes. You know the ones with the cheesy music?" Shane said.

"Think he'll make it to the Big Leagues?" Noah asked.

"Without a doubt."

"What about you? Will you play for the Red Sox someday?"

"I'd probably play for the Paw Sox first. And some other team before that... Maybe the Smelly Sox."

"Or the Lost Sox?"

They left the cages and rejoined the group in the shade of the press box. The kids tore into their brown paper bags and cartoon character lunchboxes as Lucas handed out freeze pops. Shane sat down next to Noah, chugged from his gallon of water and handed it over.

"Here, have some of mine," Shane said and offered the jug.

"No thanks."

"You need to stay hydrated."

"I guess I am thirsty." Noah accepted. "Are you helping again with workshops tomorrow?"

"Yeah, I'll be here."

After lunch was over, the Brigs threw pop flies to the kids until Hale's familiar whistle signaled the end of the clinic. Shane walked with Noah as he rounded the corner of the Rec's brick exterior. They sat together on the cement steps and watched other children hop inside trucks and minivans.

"See you, No-Kin," one of the departing boys said as he passed.

"What did he just call you?" Shane asked.

"It's just this dumb joke they have." Noah shrugged. Shane was used to ignoring the painful stuff, too, and let it go.

Noah emptied his pockets onto the steps next to him. A beer bottle cap fell out, along with a button, a crinkled dollar bill, three quarters, and an egg-shaped clump of tissues that had clearly gone through the laundry cycle a few times.

"Quite the collection," Shane said.

"Thanks." Noah found a red cough drop in the rubble, peeled the wrapper off, and popped it in his mouth.

"I almost forgot." Shane removed the crucifix necklace from the pocket of his shorts. "You left this by the pond a few weeks ago. Lucas saw it and recognized it from last summer."

Noah smiled at the necklace like he had been reunited with an old friend. "I thought I lost this." He threw it over his head and tucked the cross under his shirt. "Thank you."

"I hope I didn't scare you off that night. What were you doing out there anyway?"

He knew from Noah's face that he wouldn't get a real answer.

"Nothing." The boy got up and sat on a nearby bench, keeping his back to Shane.

"N's the middle initial on that necklace. What's your real first name?" Shane asked.

"Huh? Oh, no. Those aren't my initials. They were my Mom's."

"Is she…?"

"Yeah, she died."

"I'm sorry." Shane stood and leaned against a concrete pillar so he could face Noah. "I wear my brother's dog tags sometimes. It feels like it's a way to keep him close."

"Did he die in the army?"

"No, he's alive. His name is Troy. But when he was overseas, I'd wear them on days I really missed him."

"Did he… was he… in combat?"

"Yeah, he did a tour of duty in Iraq. He's home now."

"Must be weird to come back from that."

Noah hummed a melody that sounded like a superhero theme while Shane dwelled on the meaning of No-Kin. It was one of those nicknames that could be easily defended – Noah's full name was Noah Kinton, so No-Kin made sense. But Shane was pretty sure it was also a jab.

"So is your Dad… Who's coming to get you today?" Shane asked.

"My Grandma. Sometimes she forgets, but I'll walk if she doesn't show. You don't have to wait with me," he said in a way that was both courteous and dismissive.

"Well, if you need a ride come find me and we'll figure it out." Shane left Noah alone and returned to Hinton Fields.

The ballpark was empty except for a golf cart traveling around the warning track. Coach Hale drove the vehicle with Lexi sitting shotgun. She faced backwards, her camera aimed at Max. The star of the Brigs ran behind the cart for another scene of his athletic film. The trio buzzed by Shane and he sprinted to catch up.

"We're rolling, Shane. Stay out of frame," Lexi said.

"I will." He jogged alongside the film crew. "I just have a question for Coach."

"Shane, I'm hoping this isn't the same question you ask me before every game," Hale said.

"Coach, this isn't about short–"

"I think you're so hung up on playing shortstop that you're not seeing the big picture. What's the word for that? Lexi?"

"Tunnel vision," she answered.

"Precisely." Hale steered the cart past the away team dugout.

"Coach, this isn't about shortstop." Shane jumped to the side, nearly tripping over a few car tires leftover from the obstacle course, before catching up again. "I wanted to ask if I could come back tomorrow to help with workshops."

"But you only need to supervise once a week."

"I know."

"You trying to score some brownie points?" Max asked.

"Don't talk. You're being filmed," Lexi said.

"How many minutes of me running in a circle do you realistically need?"

"Listen, Shane," Coach Hale said. "I think it's great if you want to help out more with the kids. Maybe it will do them some good."

Shane stopped moving with the cart when he caught a glimpse of Hale's smile. It felt like a knowing wink, expressing what Hale couldn't say aloud.

Maybe it will do you some good, Shane.

CHAPTER FIVE

"The Understudy"

Shane was the only rider on the path, so he moved his bike in semicircles instead of a straight line. A crescent moon was over the coast and the bright sliver caught his eye. Shane drifted over a sand patch and crashed onto the beach. His first reaction was to make sure no one saw. Then he listened to the waves pulsing in a slow rhythm before checking his left arm. Nothing felt broken, just scraped skin and fresh blood. The equipment bag he was lugging home must have cushioned his fall.

He rode back to the Henson house and jumped off the bike when he arrived in the driveway. It plummeted across the yard and crashed into the work shed.

"Oh, he botches the dismount. That will cost him some points with the judges," Max said from behind him.

Shane turned around and saw his teammate sitting with the Henson family at the outside table. They all had purple-stained plates before them from a half-eaten blueberry pie. "Hey there."

"Come sit with us," Marie said. "Do you want a slice?"

"No thanks." He sniffed his breath, worrying they would smell the alcohol on him if they didn't already know he was drunk from his entrance.

He tucked his dog tags under his shirt before he walked over.

Shane sat next to Marie and dropped his bag on the ground. He unbuckled his chinstrap and removed his helmet.

"Do you want some pie? Or we have…" Marie trailed off as she saw the fresh wound on Shane's arm. "Did you get hurt in your game?"

"I fell off Mildred," he explained.

Marie was taken aback. "Is she your…?"

"My bike," Shane clarified. "Well, it's Fred's bike. My buddy Lucas came up with that name."

"How is that relic treating you?" Fred asked.

"Shane, you should put hydrogen peroxide on your arm," Marie said.

"I will later. Hey, did Max tell you guys about my colossal goof in the game tonight?"

"I think Shane's exaggerating," Max said.

"No, I'm not. We were fine 'til the ninth. Then I had to dive for a fly ball and it went right by my glove. The other team scored two runs, so we lost."

"There's another game tomorrow, man."

"Not if I don't do my laundry tonight." Shane motioned to the bag next to him. "Or I'll be playing in my bathrobe."

"I washed some of your clothes today," Marie said.

"You didn't have to do that."

"I'm afraid I did. That pile in your room looked like it was about to start walking around the house," she said with a laugh.

"Thank you." He was still upset with her comments about the military last week, but it was hard to stay mad when she cared for his wellbeing.

"I can do your game clothes now," Marie offered.

"Only if you let me do the dishes."

"I won't argue with that." Marie brought Shane's bag inside the house while Lexi retrieved her laptop that rested on a deck chair.

"Ooh, are we watching the movie now?" Fred said.

"It's not a movie, Dad," Lexi corrected him.

"Whatever. Video. Do you know about this, Shane? Lexi made a movie for the Brigs' website."

"Let's put it on." Shane leaned across the table to turn up the computer's volume.

"This better be my big break," Max said and massaged Lexi's back.

She pressed play on the clip and vignettes of Max filled the screen. The video featured a conditioning session at the gym, BP in the cages at Hinton Fields, and a solo homer at an away game. An instrumental version of Kendrick Lamar's "GOD." played in the background as snippets from an interview with Max served as the narration. At the end, it showed him volunteering at Burnsdale High's summer school and helping his host family cook dinner.

"Lex, this is killer," Shane said.

"Don't sound so surprised."

"You did a great job with it," Fred added.

"Thanks. It makes it easy when the talent is exceptional." She rubbed Max's arm.

"I like that it's more than a highlight reel," Max said. "You actually get to know me a little."

"Lexi, are you making more of these?" Shane asked. "Featuring other players?"

"We'll see."

●   ●   ●

A narrow staircase led him to Lexi's renovated basement lair. Shane descended then rhythmically knocked on the door to accompany the music he heard playing.

Lexi had to push the door open, its wood jammed from the late June humidity. She waited for Shane to explain his presence, but he just stood there admiring her small nose, her emerald eyes, and the sticks that poked through her hair bun.

"What's up, Shane?"

"I can't sleep," he said. "Do you want to watch a movie?"

"Hmmm... How about a short TV show?"

"Deal." Shane entered, moving past the queen bed where her laptop was open. He checked the screen and saw the song playing was "Strange Mercy" by St. Vincent.

Lexi's bookshelf was crammed with paperbacks and her college graduation cap sat atop the highest pile. A poster of the Beatles' *Revolver* artwork was taped above her bed with decorative quilts covering most of the walls to hide the drab look of the cement.

Shane sunk into the pillows of a burgundy sofa on the opposite side of the space. With a lighter in one hand and something that resembled a joint in the other, Lexi sat beside him.

"Scooby Snacks?" Shane asked.

"It's lavender. This hippie girl at school gave it to me before finals to mellow me out. It might help you sleep."

"I'm game to try."

Lexi sampled the herbal cigarette first. "It's like smoking a candle." She handed it off to Shane.

"It smells nice." He took a hit and placed it in a ceramic bowl on her dresser. "So how come Max's video is Oscar-worthy and our interview was like TMZ hopping out of the bushes?"

"You're not being fair."

"*I'm* not being fair? Why didn't you just tell me you wanted to talk about Calloway? You didn't have to blindside me."

"I'm sorry for how that went down. I had to rush. The other interns left early that night. But you didn't have to throw a tantrum."

"You're right. I'm sorry I pushed your gear over."

"Truce?"

They made the peace official with a handshake.

"You liked Max's video?" Lexi asked.

"Yeah, you should have interviewed *me* for it. I would've given you a good quote about him."

"What would you have said?" Lexi held out her fist to Shane, a pretend microphone.

Shane leaned in to speak: "The self-confidence and charisma Max has in himself sets the tone for the whole team. The way he believes in himself, it gives the rest of us permission to do the same."

He kept his head low as he awaited a follow-up question that never came. His lips were only inches from her fingers. He wanted to lean in and kiss them, but Lexi sprung off the couch.

"You should go ice that arm," she said, hovering by her bookshelf and pretending to search for a title.

"You're right. Good night." He left the basement, the stairs groaning as he went.

●　　　●　　　●

Shane folded his St. Francis Falcons jersey with caution and zipped up his sports bag slowly like the clothes inside were delicate heirlooms. He had just finished his first week practicing as the youngest member of his high school's Varsity Baseball Team.

The older boys in the locker room doused themselves with body spray. Shane eyed their muscles and their chest hair. He was eavesdropping on the social plans of the upperclassmen when a booming voice cut through the chatter.

"My fucking arm!" Coach Calloway said as he stormed into the changing area. "This is what you all have to look forward to in your forties. Your whole body falls apart." Calloway moved down the line of boys while Shane walked in the opposite direction, hoping to leave unnoticed.

"Freshman. Get me an ice pack."

Shane was a sophomore, but he knew Calloway could only be addressing him. "Where are they?"

"Where do you usually keep frozen things?"

Shane darted his eyes around like one of the lockers was going to have a freezer compartment installed in it.

"In my office," Calloway said. "Jesus, they get dumber every year."

Shane ran to Calloway's workspace and found an ice pack inside the mini-fridge. He came back and was so jittery on the handoff that he dropped the pack on the floor. Calloway smacked Shane's ass when he picked it up.

"Here you go." Shane looked up to see the hardened and angular face of his coach.

"Thanks, Frosh." Calloway applied the ice pack to his arm. "Got a girlfriend?"

"Not right now."

"You ever get in a fight?"

"No."

"What's your name again?"

"Shane."

"Shane," Calloway repeated it like an unfamiliar word. "What position do you want to play, *Shane*?"

"Shortstop."

"What have you learned so far this week?"

"Drew's been showing me some stuff about –"

"*Stuff*? Don't say stuff. That's an Emma word."

"Who's Emma?"

"My twelve-year-old daughter," Calloway said. "*Stuff*. Makes you sound like an idiot."

"Sorry, I – "

"Don't apologize. Just don't say it again."

"I won't."

"You sneak dip when you play? You know we don't allow that." Calloway stretched his arm high with the ice pack still in place.

"I don't mess with that stuf – I mean, I don't," Shane said.

"Ever tried it?"

"Once. It made me sick."

"How many chin-ups can you do?"

"Not a lot."

"Good answer."

Calloway led Shane over to the cylindrical metal bar in the doorway of his office.

"My Mom's waiting outside," Shane said.

"You want to run home to Mommy? Right after you do a chin-up for me."

The Varsity boys formed a crowd around Calloway's office to watch. They murmured to each other, but Shane couldn't discern words out of the cacophony.

Shane grasped the bar with sweaty palms. Before he began he noticed Calloway's gaze locked onto his body. The moment he tried to lift up he felt his hands slipping. Laughter came from the older boys as Shane pushed his legs against the doorframe for support.

"That doesn't count," Calloway said. "Again."

Shane stared at his coach while the volume of his snickering teammates increased.

"They're laughing at you," Calloway said. "How does that make you feel?"

"Not good," Shane said.

"So try it again."

"I can't."

"Why not?"

"I don't have the upper body strength."

His coach got close and whispered into Shane's ear: "You're stronger than you know."

Shane was surprised by the encouragement and the genuine look of belief on his coach's face. He placed his hands around the bar and attempted to pull himself up for a second time. After another short struggle he let himself fall to the ground. He stood there frozen, afraid to leave without permission.

"Show's over. See you guys tomorrow," Calloway said and the mob of teenage boys moseyed out.

"That was just sad," one of the seniors said.

Calloway folded his arms and wore a quizzical expression. "It's not too late for you to switch back to JV."

"If you want to cut me, then just do it."

"What do *you* want?"

"To stay on Varsity."

"With these little things?" Calloway pinched the boy's thin biceps.

Shane stared at the clay colored floor and shrugged his shoulders.

Don't let him see you cry.

"Do you think you could get strong?"

"I can try." Shane used his shirtsleeve to wipe the corners of his eyes.

"Good. You need to be able to do ten chin-ups consecutively by the end of this season. Understood?"

When he saw Calloway's arm coming at him, he jumped backwards, but his coach was not launching any sort of attack.

"Easy there." Calloway laughed at the way Shane flinched. He brought his hand to the top of the boy's head and ruffled his hair. "I'm gonna have some fun with you, kiddo."

CHAPTER SIX

"Brother of Mine"

Shane pressed his face against the Henson's kitchen table. The hangover was clinging on even after a hot shower and a big breakfast. He scratched the back of his neck, revealing the scrapes on his arm.

Idiot. If you had injured your arm buzzed biking…

His bag was packed on the floor with game clothes inside. There was a hand-written note from Marie on top of the clean laundry that read *Go Brigs*. He wanted to rest until Lucas came to pick him up for workshops, but someone was calling the landline. His headache worsened with each ring, so he got up from the table and answered the phone.

"Henson Residence," he mumbled.

"Shane? Is that you? It's Robin Calloway."

Damn it.

"Mrs. Calloway. How are you?"

"I'm okay. Is now a good time to talk?"

"Of course. I'm sorry I didn't get back to you before –"

"It's okay."

"And I'm sorry about… Mike's passing. I haven't even sent a

card."

"The cards are too much. I think I have it together then I read one and I'm a mess again." She cleared her throat, warding off the grief she had just mentioned. "The strangest thing is that people didn't know we were planning to separate."

"I didn't know that." Shane's gaze traveled to the driveway. He hoped Lucas would show up soon and save him from the call.

"We hadn't been the same. It started about a year ago, when Emma and me came back from visiting my sister in Seattle. That was when you guys were coming up on the State Championship. Did Mike ever mention anything that was troubling him?"

"We just talked about baseball."

"But he was obsessed with you, Shane. I found his day-planner from last year and there were whole pages about you. Notes on your game film, workout regimens he created for you."

"Yeah, that's what I mean. It was always baseball with us. We didn't talk about personal things."

"But there's a note in here about a day in April, it was during the same week me and Emma were away, it says 'Dinner with Shane.' Did you end up coming over here?"

"No." Shane's voice grew harsh as a wave of nausea rushed over him.

"I'm sorry to pry," Robin said. "But I don't have a lot of information."

"Information about what?"

"I'm trying to figure out what really happened the night he died."

"I don't understand... Mrs. Calloway...? Are you still there?"

"I shouldn't say this but... There was a picture of you on Mike's phone. Do you know the one I'm talking about?"

Country music and horn honks came from outside as Lucas pulled in the driveway. "My ride just got here. I gotta –"

"Is there another time we can talk?" she asked.

"Sorry. I don't know. Bye." Shane placed the phone back on the receiver and idled at the counter.

The rattle of the screen door snapped him back to the moment. He turned and saw Lucas enter the house.

"Dude. Can you not hear me honking out there? You're holding up the other guys."

"Who else needed a ride?" Shane peeked out the window and saw the sedan's backseat was full of little green dudes. "Very funny." He grabbed his gear and they left.

"You hit the bottle last night?" Lucas asked as they walked to the car.

"Is it that obvious?" Shane went for shotgun and wiped crumbs off the seat.

"You need to get your act together, man." Lucas fastened his seatbelt. "Can't be puking at the damn youth clinics. It's not a good look."

"What are you? My life coach? Latching onto my career 'cause yours is –"

"Oh, that's how it's going to be? Would you rather ride your rickety bike four miles to the Rec right now? 'Cause I don't have to give you a ride."

"I didn't mean it." Shane hid his face with his hands. "I feel like shit."

"If I'm overbearing it's because you still have a shot at making it big. And right now you're not acting like it." Lucas' tone was casual, like he was more concerned with backing the car out of the driveway than getting through to Shane. "And I don't like people throwing their displaced anger at me."

"You're right. I'm sorry."

"Buckle up, Boo Boo."

The nickname let Shane know they were okay. He followed orders and put on his seatbelt as Lucas drove the car down a tree-lined back road. He nodded off for a few minutes but awoke when they passed the Town Green, the site of Marie's Peace Garden.

"You know anyone in the service?" Shane asked.

"One of my buddies back home is a recruiter. What about you?"

"My brother Troy. He's in the army. He was in Iraq for ten months but he's back in Oregon now."

"Is he doing okay?"

"He's tried to get counseling through the VA but there are all these hoops he has to jump through to even get an appointment."

Shane studied Main Street as Lucas stopped at a traffic light. A long line of families formed outside a breakfast diner. "This one morning me and Troy were at our Mom's house, eating cereal together," Shane said. "The news was on in the background. And you know how they have that bar at the bottom of the screen? There was this little fact scrolling by about twenty-two veterans a day committing suicide, while the newscasters blabbered over footage of these farm pigs that had run onto a highway somewhere, jamming up traffic."

Lucas saw Shane was curled against the car door like it was a sofa. The truck behind them honked its horn since the light had changed to green. "People don't want to hear it, man." Lucas hit the gas.

"Yeah and nobody threw any parades for Troy when he came back to Astors... But I got the cover of the paper when I signed to GSU."

Lucas muted the radio as commercial blared.

"But the worst part is the assumptions people make," Shane said.

"Like who?"

"Mrs. Henson, my host parent. She practically called Troy an idiot for enlisting."

"She said that about your brother?"

"No. I told her I had a friend back home that was in the army. I didn't say it was my brother."

"Why did you lie?" Lucas turned the car into the Rec Center's parking lot and pulled into an open spot. He saw Shane go for his bag like he was about to exit the vehicle. "Hold up, Boo Boo. We're not done here."

"Where did that name come from?"

"For real. Why didn't you tell the Hensons about Troy?"

Shane reclined in the chair again. "I don't know. But it's too late to tell them now."

"No it's not. They need to know you come from a military family."

Two guys banged on the car windows from outside. Then they climbed onto the windshield and caressed the hood. It took Shane a second to see that it was J.J. and Matt.

Jose Junior, or J.J. for short, was an outfielder for the Brigs and he was never far from his smartphone. Sometimes he even snuck it in the dugout to peruse dating apps. Matt, the team cynic and second baseman, looked older than his years and often sounded disillusioned as he mumbled through his beard.

Lucas held his horn down. The monotone beep made the troublesome duo scurry. "I'm sorry, Shane. I thought we'd have time to talk."

"No, I'm sorry for unloading all that on you."

"Hey, it's like farts. It's way worse to hold them in than it is to just let them out."

"Thanks for the wisdom, Lucas." Shane pointed to the little green dudes in the back. "Should we crack a window for them?"

Lucas patted his friend on the shoulder. "I think they'll be okay."

CHAPTER SEVEN

"All We Know Is War"

Re: Purple Planet June 29 (1 day ago)
Troy Monoghan

Hey Shane,

Mom told me it's family weekend out there. I wish we could be there for it.

Sorry for the poor image quality of the photo I attached, it's a picture of a picture. I found it when I was cleaning my room. Remember the game we would play? The Purple Planet. I was an astronaut that had gone off course and you were an alien protecting your world. One time I tried to declare a truce and you just kept your gun pointed right at me. I said something like "Don't you know what surrender is on this planet?" Then you screamed, "All we know is war!"

Call me when you get a chance.

Love you,
Troy

•   •   •

The fans motioned their arms at Shane in hopes of catching his eye. He was alone for Family Night, so he tossed free t-shirts into the packed stands and watched his teammates with their loved ones. Roman delivered hot dogs to his elderly host parents on Spectator's Hill. Sam Katzman, a taciturn pitcher for the team, invited his uncle to come and had the man share stories of his time in the Minors with the bullpen. Max stood on the warning track and introduced his parents to Lexi when a familiar song came from the press box speakers. It was Frank Ocean's "Strawberry Swing" and Shane had asked Lexi to include it in her pre-game playlist. She smiled as Shane bobbed his head to the music, but Max's brow furrowed from the way her face lit up.

Wind swept over the ballpark while guys from both teams lined up for the national anthem. Shane eyed the sidelines again and saw a kid waving to him from the adjacent basketball court. Once he squinted, he saw it was Noah who was saying hello.

The boy gave a parting head nod before returning to the hoops. Shane went to take his place with the crew, feeling less alone as a pink skyline sank over the field.

•   •   •

Most of the team had already left the locker room to be with their families, but Shane and Lucas were still on the bench lacing up their sneakers.

"Your screen's flashing again." Lucas pointed to the flip phone in Shane's open locker. "Did someone call that gizmo while you were in the shower?"

"It's probably my –" A bat clanked against the floor and startled Shane. He shot up as J.J. and Matt strut in, exaggerating their movements with post-win swagger.

"We're going to Dairy Queen," J.J. said.

"I'm buying Lucas' mom a banana split," Matt joked.

"That's not even funny," Lucas replied.

"Wait, give me a minute. I'll think of something using cherry," Matt said.

Shane reached for his phone and held it close while a voicemail from his mom played: "Hi Shane. I know this was Family Night there so I wanted to call."

"Shane, are you coming to DQ?" J.J. asked.

"I miss all your music," Jenny said on the message. "It's too quiet in the house without you this summer."

"It's not my fault your mom's so hot." Matt scratched at his beard.

J.J. tapped Shane on the shoulder. "Are you coming or not?"

"Can't you see I'm on the fucking phone?" Shane chucked it in his locker and rose from the bench. "I don't hassle you when you sneak Tinder swipes in the dugout."

"Yikes. Chill out."

"So aggressive," Matt said. "Maybe you should've been the one to join the army."

How do they know about Troy?

Shane shot an incredulous stare at Lucas, who was leading J.J. and Matt down the hall.

"That's enough out of you goons," Lucas said.

"We just want to get ice cream with you, Shane." J.J. yelled from the hall. "We just want to watch you eat soft serve."

"I'll meet you two out front." Lucas came back to the bench for his things.

"Hey." Shane tugged on his teammate's arm before he could go. "Did you tell them Troy was in the army?"

"I didn't think it was a secret."

"It's not... I just –"

"My family's waiting outside. Do you want to come to Dairy Queen?"

"I don't want ice cream," Shane snapped.

"Well, sorry for inviting you." Lucas lifted the neglected bat off the floor and placed it in Shane's open bag. "Will you put this back for us?"

"Yeah, Luke. Whatever."

"You always need something to bitch about. If that's me tonight, so be it."

Once he was alone, Shane restarted the message from his mom and noticed concern in her voice at the end: "There's something I need to talk to you about and I don't want to leave it on your voicemail. So call me back later. I'll be up. Love you."

•　　•　　•

Shane sat in the Henson's kitchen and made a game of flipping his cap onto the table. He heard approaching footsteps outside the house. Whoever came in would see he had been crying, but he lacked the will to rise from his chair.

Fred entered and switched on the overhead lamp. It always took a few minutes for the bulb to fully shine, so the light stayed soft and yellow.

"Shane? Why are you sitting in the dark?" Fred moved toward the table with a broken baseball bat in his hands. He leaned it against the wall.

"Do you know where Lexi is?" Shane asked.

"Max's family took her out for dinner."

"And Marie?"

"She's at some function." Fred sat across from Shane. "Did something happen at your game?"

"The game was fine. We won." He flipped the cap a few more times. "It's my brother Troy... Did I ever mention he was in the army?"

"No."

"I don't tell people. I don't know why, but I don't."

"What's going on with him?"

"He was about to be all finished. He did his tour of duty and his four years were almost up. But my mom just told me that he voluntarily reenlisted... for another four years. And he'll probably deploy again soon."

"Where will they send him?"

"Maybe Iraq again."

"That's a lot to process." Fred pointed to the bottom half of the broken bat. "So what happened here?"

Shane saw there were specks of soil mixed in with the splinters of wood. "It was like it was taunting me."

"What was?"

"Marie's garden; the Peace Garden."

Fred's eyes became occupied like he was attempting to solve a complicated math equation. "Why were you even there?"

"My Mom left a voicemail first. She didn't say anything about Troy but I knew something was wrong. So I called her from the Town Green because... Marie had said how her garden was supposed to be this calm place. Then when my Mom told me about my brother... I just lost it. I trashed the whole thing."

A car's headlights brightened the kitchen.

"She's back," Fred said as he stood up. "Did anyone see you do it?"

"I don't know."

"Bring that thing to your room," Fred ordered. "Before she comes inside."

Shane carried the broken bat to the stairs but stopped when he made it halfway up. "Are you gonna tell her?"

"No," Fred said. "That's on you."

CHAPTER EIGHT

"Apple McPie"

Neon signs of nail salons and liquor stores lit up the commercial strip of Burnsdale. The air reeked of fast food as Max advanced in the drive thru line. He had picked up Shane and Lucas in his host parent's jeep for a dinner of cheap takeout.

"I don't know, Lucas. It doesn't look like they have apple pie," Max said as he stopped the car by the menu board.

"They don't make them back in Astors." Shane sat shotgun and noticed the bumper in front of them had a Burnsdale Brigs warship sticker on it.

"It isn't even on the menu." Max pointed to the pictures of burgers and chicken sandwiches, but no dessert options were in sight.

"'Cause they're like a secret bonus for loyal customers," Lucas said from the backseat. "They're called Apple McPies now."

"You're messing with me. You just want me to sound like an idiot when the person takes our order."

"Hi, what can I get for you tonight?" a voice asked over the intercom.

"Max, I want seven Apple McPies," Lucas whispered.

"Shut up."

"Order already," Shane said.

Max stuck his head out the window and spoke into the intercom. "Hi. I need three #1 meals, all with medium fries and cokes."

"Does that complete your order?"

"Uh..." Max felt Lucas nudge his shoulders from the back. "Is apple pie still on the menu?"

An achingly long silence transpired. Shane laughed at himself as he realized how much anticipation he felt.

"You mean Apple McPie?" the voice answered.

Lucas clapped his hands together.

"Yes. Three of those please," Max said.

"Comes to $28.62. Second window."

Max checked Lucas' expression in the rearview mirror. "Man, wipe that smile off your face or I'm driving away without the food."

"'You do not realize now what I am doing, but later you will understand,'" Lucas recited.

"You're seriously dropping some scripture on me over an Apple McPie?"

They got their food and relocated to a parking lot by Burnsdale Harbor. Tourists clothed in pastel colors strolled the docks and a couple seagulls circled overhead. The birds received no scraps as the boys feasted.

"You guys see that girl on the bench?" Lucas said.

"She's cute," Max said. "You should go talk to her."

"Think I won't?" Lucas wiped the crumbs off his mouth and exited the jeep.

"Watch out, folks. He means business," Shane said and watched his friend approach the girl. After a quick hello, she invited Lucas to sit with her on the bench. Then Shane's head flung back as Max reversed the car.

"What are you doing?" Shane asked. "You can't leave him there."

"I just did him a favor." Max smiled as they drove away from the harbor. "Now he has to make it work."

The orange remnants of daylight dwindled as the prolonged dusk became a dark blue night. Max cruised down Main Street and slowed the jeep down when they passed the Town Green.

"You hear about this yet?" Max asked. "Mrs. Henson's new garden got destroyed by some punks."

"I hadn't heard," Shane said.

"I'm surprised you and Lexi didn't talk about it."

It was like Max knew about the charged moment he and Lexi had on her couch the week before. "We don't talk."

"What do you want to do now?" Max turned the vehicle to make a loop around the Town Green again.

"Anything but drive in circles." Shane turned his face away from the garden when he felt like his Apple McPie might come back up. He wondered if the local police were investigating the incident.

"Holy shit! Was it you? Did you kill the garden?"

"I..." Shane ducked his head down, embarrassed. "How did you know?

"Let's say it's a good thing you don't play poker." Max directed the jeep onto the coastal roads. He shut the radio off once they made it to the water. "So why'd you do it?"

"It wasn't like I planned it out," Shane said. "I was pissed about something else and the garden is where I happened to be."

"This is about your brother? I heard some of the guys talking about him."

Shane saw a ferry cutting through the calm sea. "Yeah. He reenlisted."

"You talk to him yet?"

"If we talk I'll just get mad."

"You got too much fire in you, man." Max placed one hand over his mouth and used the other to steer. "Do you see the dilemma this puts me in?"

Shane turned away from the coast and faced Max. "What dilemma?"

"Me and Lexi are dating, and it's her Mom's garden you just pillaged, and now I know it was you that did it, but Lexi doesn't know. I'm bad at secrets, man."

"Are you planning on marrying her or something? You're only here for like six weeks."

Max accelerated the jeep to pass a cyclist and continued speeding even after the rider was behind them. "I care about her and I don't want to lie."

"I shouldn't have told you any of this," Shane said.

"You didn't tell me. I figured it out."

"Whatever. Just let me out of the car."

"Fine." Max veered the jeep to the side of the road, pulling into a dirt lot. "Here you go."

Shane lingered, stunned that his bluff had been called.

"You wanted to walk home, right?" Max reached across and opened up the door for him.

Shane grunted as he unbuckled his seat belt and got out. He crossed over to walk along the shoreline and saw the jeep drive away. If he followed the coast for long enough it would lead him back to Devil's Foot. He reached for his phone, considering if he should call the Hensons for a ride. But he decided to continue his trek as the incoming tide claimed some child's forgotten sandcastle.

CHAPTER NINE

"4th of July"

Marie's fingers were covered in dirt as she arranged new plantings in the Peace Garden. She lifted her head at the squeak of brakes and saw Shane standing with his bike at the edge of the Town Green.

"Can I help?" he asked.

"I don't want you to be late for practice."

"I've got a little time." He hopped over the fencing and walked to the garden, on the way noticing American flags hanging from the streetlamps for the holiday.

They worked quietly in the sun, but the silence was a product of focus, not tension. Marie showed Shane how to tamp the soil and to water the plants at their bases. A group of German tourists went by, sounding critical as they pointed at the garden.

"Where's your crew?" Shane asked.

"I gave them the day off for the 4th. But I get antsy if I sit around."

"I know the feeling."

Marie saw Shane's hands were shaking as he patted down the dirt. "Have you been sleeping okay in Lexi's old room? Sometimes I hear you up at night."

"It's like I can't shut my mind off. I should do more stuff like this." He gestured to the earth. "How hard has it been to restart this?"

"We saved a couple plants but it's going to take a lot of work to get it back to where it was."

"I'm sorry."

"I don't think it was personal. But who knows? Small towns are strange. Maybe I offended someone."

"Mrs. Henson, I have to tell –"

The bells of a nearby church rang out for high noon.

"What were you saying, Shane?"

"Nothing." He got up and wiped his hands on his shirt. "I have to go to practice."

•   •   •

Katzman hurled his fastball from the mound. Shane tried to correct his swing once it registered the pitch was moving away from the plate, but it was too late. He missed the ball as Jermaine caught it with his outstretched arm.

"You got that one?" Jermaine lifted his mask for a check-in. The catcher for the Brigs had a red, white, and blue headband over his buzzed black hair.

"Churning butter means outside fastball," Shane said.

They had spent the practice reviewing Jermaine's new set of hand signals while rotating through the different pitchers. Shane wanted to learn the code if he made it back to shortstop. Then he could call better plays for the infield with the knowledge of both pitching and defensive signals.

"You coming to Roman's shindig tonight?" Jermaine asked.

"Am I invited?"

"You are now." The catcher put his mask back on and chucked the ball to the mound.

The next signal looked like a propeller spinning and Katzman nodded in agreement. Shane knew it was the sign for a changeup. He waited for the ball to dip then blew it out to right field.

"You're a quick learner," Jermaine said.

Someone applauded behind Shane. When he faced the stands, he saw Noah by the basketball court at the top of the hill. The boy came down to meet Shane on the warning track. He had three glow-sticks wrapped around his neck like chokers. He wore gym shorts and a heavy, gray sweatshirt.

"Noah, how are you not dying in that hoodie?"

The kid shrugged at the question.

"What's up?" Shane asked. "You just come by to say hey?"

"I have a favor to ask. There's a pickup game by the Heights before the fireworks start... And I was hoping I could use your glove."

From the stupefied face Shane made, Noah knew he might as well have asked to chop off Shane's arm and borrow it for the day.

The old, brown Spalding had been Shane's go-to glove since senior year of high school and it fit his hand like lock-and-key.

"I won't lose it," Noah said.

"What happened to *your* glove?"

"It's at my Dad's house."

"Why can't you go there and get it?"

"I don't want to bike back."

"He's your Dad. Why can't he just bring it to you?"

"He just can't, okay?" Noah snapped.

Shane walked over to the bleachers and grabbed the mitt. "You need to bring it back by eleven tomorrow morning. I have an early game."

"I'll be here."

"Don't have to worry about you stretching it out." Shane gave the boy the glove. Noah's sleeve fell down on the handoff, revealing a purple mark on his skin.

"You get in a fight with somebody?"

"What?" Noah covered his arm once he realized the bruise was in sight.

"You had a black eye the night we met," Shane said. "What were you doing sleeping by the pond anyway? How bad does... What are things like at home?"

The boy clutched Shane's glove tight and stared off into the distance.

"Noah?"

"Huh? Sorry, I spaced out." Noah retreated up the bleachers and held the mitt high. "I'll be back with this tomorrow."

•　　　•　　　•

There were thousands of people gathered along the coastal neighborhood known as The Heights. Vendors sold neon gear and pinwheels in the closed-off streets to the families anticipating the big show. Squads of high school kids flocked down from the cliffs and twenty-somethings shared beers out of red beach coolers.

The Brigs were watching from Roman's host family's house, which was close enough that the display could be seen from the front porch. But Shane saw each ember, explosion, and ripple in the night sky from his slouched position by a beachside motel. He was a sucker for fireworks and wanted a front seat to the action, even if it meant braving the crowd.

His face was painted like the American flag but the temperature was so hot the design was melting, giving him a Heath Ledger Joker look that had already scared a few small children on the strip.

The barges in Eleanor's Sound vanished in the smoky horizon after the rapid-fire finale. Shane grabbed Mildred from behind the motel once the exodus began. He rode through the exhaust fumes and clouds of cigarette smoke.

When he made it to the yellow Cape ranch a block away, he ditched Mildred in the driveway. 808 beats and joyous voices rang out from the backyard. A wooden fence enclosed the house, keeping the festivities out of sight. Shane stopped by the entrance and finished off the half pint of whiskey he carried in the drawstring bag on his back.

The burning sensation of the alcohol climbed up his chest as he went through the gate. There were twelve guys spread out across the backyard. Some of them played a game of beanbag toss while others stood around the fire-pit.

"Shane. You came," Lucas yelled and pulled him into the circle.

"I need some water," Max said. He dodged Shane and left the group.

"Wasn't sure if you would show." Jermaine tapped knuckles with Shane.

"Killer face paint," Matt said with a giggle.

"You want a drink, Shane?" Lucas offered.

"I just realized I skipped dinner."

"Roman, get this man a cheeseburger."

"I'm on it," Roman said from the deck.

"Glad you came, Shane," Dennis said. He was the first baseman for the Brigs and had stopped applying aloe to his sunburnt skin to put his hand out for a shake.

Shane avoided his teammate's lubricated palm and patted him on the shoulder instead.

"Ow." Dennis cringed. "I'm burnt there, too."

"Hey, where's Katzman? Or Cummings?" Lucas said. "Are the pitchers having their own shindig?"

Shane's head felt like it was wobbling and his stomach sounded like the site of a mild earthquake. He excused himself from the circle once Max came back. His steps were uneven as he hobbled to the back deck where Roman worked the grill.

"Grill-master-Roman over here," Shane said. "The Millers don't care we're hanging out here tonight?"

"They've been asleep for like three hours already," Roman said. "And even if they wake up they never put their hearing aids in."

Shane took a seat on the deck. His sickness softened as he watched Roman tend to the meat.

"I can bring you your food when it's done if you want to go talk to people," Roman said.

"No. It's safer up here."

"I feel you. Party talk is tough. Flipping burgers is a breeze."

They stayed in a comfortable silence until Lexi came onto the deck. Shane leapt up and gave her a hug. "Happy Fourth, Lexi."

"Hi, Shane. Did a box of crayons explode on your face?"

"I still have the kit in my bag. Will you make it look better?"

The guests formed a line on the deck as Roman served dinner. Max came up and watched Lexi as she redid Shane's facepaint.

"Lexi, where is your Dad from originally?" Shane asked.

"America. How about yours?"

"I'm sorry. I didn't mean it like –"

"I'm giving you shit. My Dad was born here. But his mother came here from Japan."

"I've never –"

"Will you quit babbling and hold still? You're going to ruin my artwork." She stood back for a moment to examine him. "You look like a little boy," she said with pride. Lexi used a wet napkin to polish Shane's cheeks while her other hand rested on his upper thigh.

Shane grew excited from her touch and needed to leave before she noticed. "Where's the bathroom?"

"The first door down the hall on your left," Roman said. "Bring the ketchup out on your way back."

Shane entered the dark house and opened the first door he came across, startling the occupants of the master bedroom.

"Roman? Is that you? Is everything alright?" Mrs. Miller said from under the covers.

"Everything's fine. I'm just looking for ketchup," Shane used a deeper register of his voice, trying to imitate Roman's nasal tone.

Mr. Miller rolled over on his side and let out a muffled fart.

Shane shut the door behind him and stumbled down the hall. He knocked over a framed photo of a young Mr. Miller in formal military gear. In the picture, the man's hair was slicked back and he wore a pensive expression. Shane hung it back up then found the bathroom.

He admired himself in the mirror for a long time, the stars in the blue pool on his forehead and the alternating stripes of red and white across his cheeks and nose. Then he removed his t-shirt and studied the collection of hairs growing on his chest.

"Why'd I come in here?" he asked his reflection.

When he returned to the deck, Roman presented him with a

cheeseburger. "Where's the ketchup, Shane?"

"That's what I forgot."

"Do you want me to do your whole body now?" Lexi laughed at Shane's exposed torso.

"I don't think we'll have time." Shane wolfed down the entire burger.

The party's playlist got choppy as a series of texts from one of J.J.'s girls kept interrupting the song.

"That's it. Shane's the DJ now." Jermaine unplugged J.J.'s phone from the speakers. "You're abusing your privileges."

Shane went over to the fire pit. The pitchers had shown up along with the older interns. The party had hit capacity while he was on the deck and the guests waited to see what song Shane would choose. "You guys in the mood for anything in particular?"

"Something ape-shit," Dennis said.

"I was telling everyone how you've got the sounds. Don't make me a liar," Jermaine said.

The fire crackled beneath Shane and when he peered up he saw the sons of summer were hungry for him to speak.

"Y'all having a good fourth?"

The crew cheered.

"You guys ready to win that championship for Hale?"

The shouts grew louder and Shane fed off the noise.

"I'm sorry it took me so long to come out of my cave... But I'm here now. Go Brigs!" Shane pressed play and a song called 'Sunbathing Animal' by Parquet Courts blared. The one note guitar line and punk drum beat kicked in and the partygoers thrashed around. Shane grinned at the madness he made.

Standing on the side of the mosh-pit was Max, his arms crossed.

"Mighty Max, Mighty Max," Shane sang as he danced his way over. "Just how long can his hot streak last?"

"Is that little jingle payback for your long walk home the other night?" Max said.

"Whatever. That was a fun four miles. It built character."

"Quit dancing for a second and actually talk to me."

"Okay." Shane settled down.

"I'm sorry I left you on the road. I came back five minutes later and I couldn't find you."

"It was good you did that. I get it now, that I put you in a tough spot with Lexi... So are we okay?"

"Of course. You're my brother."

"Brother?" Shane repeated the term like it was an unexpected promotion.

"Brother." Max hugged him.

"Brother..."

It made him think of Troy. He felt at his neck and realized the dog tags were gone and somehow he knew they had been gone for a while. Panic set in as he retraced his steps. He went by the fence and onto the deck, but there was no sign of them anywhere. Jermaine turned the music down as Shane's distress killed the collective buzz.

"Has anyone seen dog tags?" Shane yelled.

Lexi tried to hold him still, but he was already starting a second sweep of frantic searching.

"You know my Dad served," Dennis said.

"That's great, but I gotta find these tags," Shane said. "Maybe they're back at the Heights. Or they might have fallen in the grass."

The team watched Shane drop to his knees and crawl.

"Maybe it was the head banging?" Shane guessed. "Like they flew right off. I was looking at myself in the bathroom and they weren't on in there."

The Brigs stared at each other in a shared state of confusion. Lexi yanked Shane by a belt loop on his jeans and directed him into the outdoor shower.

"You two need some alone time in there?" Max asked.

"Skip it," she said. "I didn't see you coming to the rescue." Lexi stepped into the wooden cubicle and shut the door behind her.

"Why are we in this phone booth?" Shane asked from the floor of the shower.

"This is the calm-down-corner," Lexi said.

"Is that like code for time-out?"

"Let's try breathing together."

Lexi got on her knees and locked in with Shane so their inhales and exhales were synchronized.

When he leaned in to kiss her, she placed a hand on his chest. "Shane. That's not what this is."

He tried to advance again and kissed the air for a moment before he realized she had stood up.

"Don't go. I'll be good." He hugged her legs to stop her exit then fell back to the floor. "My head has bubbles in it."

"There's a game tomorrow. Why'd you get so drunk?"

"Noah, this boy from workshops, his father..." Shane still felt nervous saying it aloud even in his altered state. "I think his father is hitting him. And there's nothing I can do."

"Have you told Hale about this?"

"The same thing's going to happen to Noah. And I can't stop it from happening." Shane shed a tear. "Oh, shit. There's no crying in baseball."

He sprung from the floor to crank the showerhead and let the cold water soak him. "How do I look now?"

His makeup bled into a stream of pinks and purples. He glanced to the sky and through his blurred vision he saw a sea of constellations and heard the quick pops of fireworks. "Is the sky exploding?"

"Jesus Christ." Lexi shut the water off. "Let's get you home."

"What about Mildred?"

"I've got Fred's truck. We can throw her in the back."

He used his thumb to clean the mess from his face. His eyes stung from the chemicals, but he was relieved when he looked up and saw the stars were still in place.

CHAPTER TEN

"Calloway's House"

Shane's a twig.

He selected the twenty-pound dumbbells from the rack of free weights in the high school weight room.

I could snap him in two.

Rosco's words echoed in Shane's thoughts. Some kids were inventing hypothetical fight scenarios between different St. Francis students that day at lunch. Rosco, the captain of the football team, deemed Shane an unworthy rival for a brawl. The table laughed while Shane picked at his tater-tots and said nothing to contest the matter.

The mirrored wall of the St. Francis weight room allowed him to watch all his peers in 5th Period P.E. lift on weight machines. He knew most of the guys from Baseball or Cross Country and couldn't help but notice that they had all bulked up over the last few years. Even with the exclusive travel leagues he was a part of, and the baseball watch-lists he had earned a place on, no accolade mattered as much as the fact that he was still not jacked.

"Monoghan, how long you been playing for me?" Calloway asked from the corner of the room, clutching a clipboard of workout regimens.

"Three years." Shane exhaled through gritted teeth. He finished a set of curls then set the weights down.

"And we're still waiting on puberty to start, huh?"

The guys chuckled at the crack, but Shane was more upset that Calloway seemed to be able to read his thoughts whenever he wanted.

"And I'm still waiting on you to stop being a dick," Shane mumbled.

Calloway chucked his clipboard across the room. The sharp thud caused one student to drop the weights on the leg extension machine.

"Outside. Now." Calloway commanded.

Shane rolled his eyes as the guys made *you're-in-big-trouble* oohs. He slouched against the red lockers in the unoccupied hallway, awaiting reprimand.

"You're not acting like yourself," Calloway said. "What's going on with you?"

"My mom's been away this week. I haven't been eating well."

"Does the protein powder still feel hard on your stomach?"

Shane gave no response. He had been a victim of the tactic too many times before. In the past, he would let his guard down only to be chewed out again by Calloway moments later.

"I want to show you something." Calloway took his phone out and after a few seconds of scrolling, handed the device over. There was a picture of a pale-skinned teenage boy on the screen. He was changing his clothes in the St. Francis locker room. Shane identified the birthmark on the right shoulder as his own. It must have been sophomore year since his hair was shaggy and grown out long.

"Look how much stronger you've gotten."

"Right..."

"One day you're going to look back on how you are now and feel the same way." Calloway took his phone and returned to the weight room.

After lifting, Shane changed back into kakis and a polo shirt. His friend Kev Ralstein, who was a year younger, had the locker next to him. Shane became a mentor for Kev since the junior was slated to take over as shortstop.

"Why's Coach always riding you so hard?" Kev asked as he used the camera feature on his phone to fix his long bangs before returning to class.

Shane sighed as he tied his bootlaces. "I don't even think about it anymore."

"Hang in there, bud." Kev gave him a gentle punch on the arm then left at the sound of the sixth period bell.

Shane tried to rush by Calloway's office, but a harsh knock came from his coach's window. Shane turned and saw Calloway signaling him to enter.

"I've got class." Shane stood still by the double doors and forced his coach to come to him.

"You're probably sick of takeout." Calloway drew closer. "Why don't you come over my house for dinner this week?"

"That's alright, Coach. You don't have to feed me."

"I know Robin would like to see you. And it'd be good to spend some time with you off the field. You won't be my player for much longer." He massaged Shane's shoulder. "How's Thursday sound?"

"Uh, sure. Sounds good." A chill came over Shane while Calloway's hand slid down his arm. He pulled away and left the locker room.

"You need a pass?"

"I'll get one from Ms. Avery," Shane said as the doors closed. He rushed down the halls, forgetting to stop at Guidance on the way. His mind was still preoccupied with the photo his coach had shown him. He wondered what would have possessed the man to take it in the first place.

•   •   •

There was nothing unusual about the colonial house where the Calloway family lived, but Shane still felt a sinister energy as he waited on the front porch. The breeze that caused the budding branches to sway, the rapid pace of the gray clouds, the calls from a lone crow, and the patches of burnt grass on the front yard, they all became harbingers of dread.

Shane knew once he saw Mrs. Calloway he'd feel better about the dinner. She was a much warmer person than her husband and often brought homemade baked goods to their ballgames.

He knocked his fist against the crimson-colored stained glass on the front door. Then he saw a figure approaching through the opaque screen.

Calloway held the door open. "Good to see you, Shane. Come on in."

"I should have brought a gift or something. I'm sorry."

"Don't be silly."

The quiet inside the foyer was alarming. "Where's Mrs. Calloway?"

"It slipped my mind the other day. She took Emma with her to Seattle. They're visiting family. Just us guys tonight."

Calloway went down the hall and Shane lingered for a moment. Some unfamiliar sensation was boiling up within him. It was like nausea but he could feel it in his blood, like his whole being wanted to leave.

"Will you grab the door, Shane?"

Stop being crazy.

Shane did as his coach requested then ventured inside the home.

•　　•　　•

Steak, vegetables, and basmati rice were stacked on his plate. The dining room walls displayed a few family portraits and last year's Falcons team photo. Calloway came back with two bottles of beer. Shane was hesitant to accept, but his coach reassured him by twisting the cap off.

"You said your Mom was visiting…?"

"My brother Troy," Shane said. "He's getting this award at his base before he comes home."

"That's great." Calloway downed his beer like it was water. "Tell me who's doing dip on the team."

"That why you had me over? You want me to rat?"

"You don't have to name names, but it's happening?"

Shane confirmed with a head nod.

"Shit's disgusting," Calloway said.

"What? Don't hockey guys have bad habits?"

Calloway held up his bottle then finished it with one gulp. "You want another?" He stood from the table and went to the kitchen.

"I'm still working on this one."

"Catch up." Calloway placed a second beer next to Shane's plate despite his refusal.

"This food is all really good," Shane said. "Thanks for having me over." He sipped on his beer for a while until his cheeks felt warm and numb.

"So did I hear you took Joslyn Reid to Senior Formal?" Calloway asked.

"You heard correct."

"Are you two...?"

"Nah, Coach. It's not like that."

"Why not? She's a beautiful girl."

"She is. We're just friends though."

"You mean to tell me you ain't been getting laid?"

Shane forced a laugh. "What's it to you?"

"Guess I saw you in a different light, that's all."

"What is that supposed to mean?"

Calloway shrugged. They ate in silence for the rest of the meal.

"I'll clean this up later," Calloway said. "Let's watch some game film."

"I thought this was just dinner."

"Come on. You always learn something from it."

They walked toward the living room and Shane paused by an old photograph of Calloway in his twenties. He was on the ice and clad in hockey gear. "When was this?"

"Mid-nineties I think. That was my AHL team. Furthest I got."

"Why do you coach baseball instead of hockey?"

"It worked out St. Francis needed a baseball coach when I moved here." Calloway continued down the hall.

A chin-up bar installed in the living room doorway threatened

Shane as he passed underneath.

"How many of those can you do these days?" Calloway asked.

"I don't know. Ten, maybe."

The painful memory from sophomore year in the locker room returned to Shane's mind as he waited to see if Calloway would make him hop up on the bar. "How many do you do?"

Calloway latched onto the bar and completed twenty without a hint of strain.

"Showoff," Shane said.

They settled in the living room where a flat screen TV hung on the wall. Calloway hovered by the liquor cabinet and poured two glasses of scotch. Shane accepted the drink and eased back onto the leather sofa. His coach readied footage from their last game, fast-forwarding to one of Shane's at-bats, then playing it in slow motion. The analysis seemed sincere and thorough, but Shane just nodded along as he tuned out Coach's words.

Calloway switched the television off and tossed the remote onto an ottoman. "Are you even listening?"

"Sorry," Shane said. "I'm tired."

"College ball is coming up and I'm worried you're not ready."

"Not ready?"

"You're not strong enough. I put a lot of time and energy into developing you the last few years. It's started to feel like a bad investment. 'Cause now the next level is here, and I don't know…"

Shane let his head fall back against the wall. He wiped away tears from his eyes. "Why are you saying this to me?"

"It can be hard to hear the truth."

"If I'm not ready, then why did I get signed to one of the best college programs in the country?"

"Because they can use you to sell tickets and merchandise and get more kids to come to their school. But they don't care what happens to you once you leave. I want you to make it to the Majors. And if you don't change your approach soon, I don't see that happening."

Shane's mind went blank as he pressed his palms against his face.

"Don't be mad at me for being honest." Calloway touched Shane's knee then rubbed the joint. "We can still have sessions this summer."

Shane froze as he looked down and saw Calloway's hand travel up his thigh and towards his lap.

"We'll get you ready."

Shane shot up from the couch after Calloway grabbed his groin. "What are you doing?"

His coach had no answer. He just stared at him from the couch.

"I... I'm... I gotta go." Shane turned to leave.

"Don't confuse what that was. You're drunk." Calloway sprung from the couch and blocked Shane's path. "I can give you a ride."

"I'll be fine." Shane felt his mother's car keys in his pocket and waited for his coach to step aside.

"I can't let you drive," Calloway said, remaining still.

"I'll walk then. Just let me through."

"Don't make a fool of yourself. There's a guest room upstairs you can sleep in." Calloway tried to guide Shane to the staircase but got his arm swatted away.

"Bet you'd like that."

Calloway lunged at Shane and backed him into a corner. Shane held his breath, afraid to let it hit his coach's imposing face. Then he felt the car keys in his pocket. He pushed down on the circular button he knew would trigger the vehicle's alarm. The harsh horns and flashing lights from outside made Calloway step back.

Shane sprinted down the hall once his path was clear. He turned back to see if his coach was following then ran face first into a doorframe. His vision went fuzzy as he saw dots dance in circles, but he kept moving, tripping down the front steps and into the driveway.

The pain of his collision was sinking in as he shut the alarm off and got in the car. He dropped his keys when he saw Calloway watching him from inside.

"Fuck. Fuck. Fuck."

Shane picked them up, started the car, and pulled away from the house. He drove under the flickering streetlights of Astors until he made it back to his neighborhood.

It was dark by his home. He forgot to switch the front light on before he left, something his mother always remembered to do for him. Inside he caught his breath, then checked his reflection in the mirror. A trail of blood had formed across his face, traveling from his nostrils all the way to his right ear lobe. He lifted his hand to his cheek.

CHAPTER ELEVEN

"Into the Fog"

The space where he woke was unfamiliar at first, but he knew he was in Lexi's room once he saw the wine-colored couch cushions. He looked around to make sure she wasn't in the basement before he stood up with morning wood.

His upper lip felt wet. He put his hand to his nostrils, blood coating his fingers.

He rushed to the bathroom, clenching his nose on the way up. In the mirror, he saw a red stream run from his cheek back to his earlobe. He could only laugh at the visceral way the dream had left its mark on his morning.

The nosebleed subsided in a couple minutes. He washed up with warm water as the initial hints of a hangover snuck up on him.

"Wait. What time is it?"

The clock in the living room read 11:37.

Game starts at noon. You were supposed to be on the field like half an hour ago.

He hurried back to the basement for his things. His phone buzzed with an incoming call from Lucas. "What's up?"

"Where are you?" Lucas said. "Did you oversleep?"

Shane grabbed his shoes and clothes. "Yeah, I can still make it though."

"You want me to come get you?"

"No. I've got Mildred."

"The lineup's posted. You're at shortstop."

"Perfect." He ended the call, did two stairs at a time up to the second floor, and ran to his room. In the middle of stuffing his bag with game clothes, sliding shorts, and packs of bubble gum, he realized he was missing one crucial item. He had lent his glove to Noah the day before.

●　　　●　　　●

Shane spotted the Nauset Admirals warming up in the outfield. If it weren't for the crimson accents on their jerseys, their gray away uniforms would have blended into the fog hanging over Hinton Fields. He scoped out the bleachers, only a few fans had shown up with the overcast weather and none of them were Noah.

Shane slid his hand into the black Rawlings glove he had been using for the outfield. It was still resistant to his fingers' commands, even though he had used some shaving cream to break in the leather. He walked to the dugout and read the whiteboard: Seventh in the lineup, 18 Monoghan SS.

He checked the perimeter of the park once more for Noah. On his loop, he passed the bullpen and saw Brigs pitcher Robbie Cummings practicing his curveball with Jermaine catching for him.

"Hit pause for a second," Jermaine said. "I need to do some squats."

Cummings responded by spitting out an abrasive loogie. He was a chatterbox off the mound, but the only way he communicated during game time was with head nods or adjusting the intensity of his spit. Shane tried to get into shortstop mode as he remembered that Cummings didn't strike guys out that often, but threw pitches that turned into easy fly outs or grounders.

The bike ride and the humidity made Shane perspire. His cap seemed to tighten around his skull, so he went to the batting cages, sensing he'd be ill soon. He knelt by the chain link fence and vomited. The back of his throat burned and his teeth felt grimy as he heard footsteps scurrying past. It was Gus-the-batboy.

"Man, you must be nervous about playing shortstop," the boy said, keeping his distance.

"Yeah..." Shane kicked dirt over the puddle of puke. "You seen Noah around?"

"He was here a while ago, but we couldn't find you anywhere."

"Did he leave my glove?"

Gus had already run off. Across the field, Shane saw Coach Hale conversing with Max.

There goes my chance at shortstop.

"Hold on," Shane yelled. He ran to the spot on the warning track where Hale and Max spoke. "Am I too late?"

"I was seeing if Max would be willing to cover for you," Hale said. "Does he need to?"

"No, sir. I want to play."

"I won't always be here to bail you out," Max said and jogged to the bench.

"Look, Coach. I overslept. I totally –"

Hale raised his hands to halt Shane's explanation. "We can talk about it later. I just need to know if you're ready for this."

Hale made intense eye contact, making Shane guess the game had some secret significance. But he still nodded his head in affirmation. "Yeah, Coach. I'm ready."

Shane spotted a group of middle-aged men settle down in the stands. They scribbled into oversized notebooks and adjusted buttons on their speed radar guns. It was easy to figure out who they were with attendance so low.

Scouts.

Shane didn't know what organizations they worked for, but they had come to find the future stars of the sport.

Yeah, Coach. I'm ready.

•   •   •

The space he occupied on the field seemed like sacred ground after being deprived of shortstop for so long. He wished he could play naturally, but he found himself second-guessing each one of Jermaine' hand signals, botching communication with Matt on who would cover second, and even overanalyzing the mild breeze that came off the nearby harbor.

A hitter for Nauset whacked a bouncy grounder towards Shane. He shimmied up the field to align with the projectile and made the simple catch. His grip became awkward as he launched to Matt.

Uh oh.

He picked up the dropped baseball and tossed it to his teammate. The Brigs got one out, but Shane's blunder cost them the chance at a double play.

Nice going. I'm sure the scouts will make big notes about that one.

Shane kept replaying his mistake as Cummings struck out an overzealous Nauset batter.

Don't snowball right now. Stay in the game.

The next Admiral hit the first pitch Cummings threw. The ball soared and started a slow drop that would land somewhere between Shane and Lucas. Shane waved his arms to signal his friend he had it covered while Lucas did the same thing.

"I got it!" Shane barked.

The ball plopped into Shane's glove as he dodged a collision with Lucas.

"What the fuck, man? I had it," Shane said.

"Easy, compadre." Lucas put his hands up in surrender. "Just wanted to make sure."

The players cleared the diamond for the next inning. Shane stormed into the dugout, chucking his glove against the batting helmets. The other guys let him have the bench to himself so he could cool off.

"Do you want to talk?" Hale asked and sat next to Shane.

"No."

"Do you want to keep playing?"

"No. You should put Max in." Shane dropped his head and saw a dusting of sunflower seeds across the dirty dugout floor.

"Okay. I'll let him know," Hale said.

"It was a mistake for me to play today."

"That's how you learn, right?"

"But what if you keep making the same mistakes?" Shane lifted his head and saw Hale scrambling to find an answer. "Sorry. I can go tell Max he's up."

•　　　•　　　•

Marie was filling out paperwork at the kitchen island when Shane came in the house. He turned the corner and saw the living room was dark for Fred's viewing of an old cowboy movie.

"You like Westerns?" Shane asked over the gunshot sound effects.

"It's almost been a week now," Fred said as he kept his eyes glued to the TV.

"I know. I tried to tell her yesterday but –"

"Rip off the band-aid already, kid."

Shane dropped his bag by the couch then walked over to Marie's kitchen workspace.

"We had BLTs," she said. "I left the bacon out for you."

"Thanks." Shane studied the landscape designs, payment invoices, and client files spread over the surface.

"We were worried about you last night. Why didn't you tell me you had plans to stay out when you saw me at the garden?"

"I should have. I'm sorry."

"So where'd you stay?"

"I'm confused now," Shane said. "I slept here last night."

"But I went to wake you up for your game and you weren't in your room this morning."

"That's 'cause I slept in the basement."

"Oh…"

Shane saw Marie's dumbfounded face as different scenarios flooded her mind. "Mrs. Henson, I promise, me and Lexi, we're not... It's not like that. Nothing happened."

Right?

"I'm just glad you were somewhere safe," she said.

Shane put bread in the toaster then reached for the bacon. The meat was sitting on a plate lined with newspapers. He unveiled the running ink of an article about the Peace Garden's destruction that was sopping up the bacon's grease.

Marie gathered up her papers. "You know... the light down here makes my eyes hurt."

Shane thought about asking her to stay. He knew Fred was listening from the living room and that Mr. Henson didn't want to keep a secret from his wife for much longer. But Shane had already fumbled so many things over the last few hours. He stayed quiet as Marie went upstairs, hoping the truth could wait one more day.

CHAPTER TWELVE

"Et in Arcadia"

He raised his head from the ground, releasing from the hamstring stretch, and saw Lexi jog down the Henson's drive. She was wearing her gym clothes, her face flushed from a run.

"Morning," she said.

"Morning. I was looking for you in the house to see if you wanted to go running. Guess you beat me to it."

"Can we talk before you go?" Lexi sat down in the front yard, catching her breath. "What do you remember about the night of the 4th?"

Shane chuckled. "You sound like you're a detective."

"Well, we didn't get a chance to talk yesterday. So the 4th... Things are hazy for you?"

"I don't remember going to bed in your room," he said. "I don't even remember leaving Roman's. I didn't do anything... Like, try to force –"

"No. Not at all. The only reason I had you sleep in the basement is because I was worried you might puke in your sleep."

"Thanks for looking out."

"But… you don't remember… the dream you were having?"

I was back in Calloway's house.

"Why?" Shane asked. "Was I talking in my sleep?"

"You woke up in the middle of the night and freaked," she said. "You kept crying and shaking. I tried to calm you down but it was like you were in a trance."

"I'm sorry you had to see me like that."

"You don't need to apologize." Lexi used the back of her hand to wipe the sweat off her forehead. "It doesn't have to be me, but you have to talk to someone about whatever's going on."

She watched Shane fiddle with the bunny-ear knots on his sneakers. "Hello? Earth to Shane. Did I get through?"

He kept his face low. "It was just a nightmare."

He heard Lexi scoff before she pushed off the ground and went into the house.

•   •   •

Shane found refuge from the heat under the bleachers. He hoped he might discover Troy's missing dog tags among the Cracker Jack cartons and empty Gatorade bottles, but there was only litter on the ground.

"You hiding from something under there?" Hale asked as his white kicks came into Shane's line of sight.

"Huh? All this trash was bugging me." Shane noticed a crumpled program from the game against Waterford a few weeks back. He added it to his collection bag.

"Max came by earlier. He said you two had quite the workout this morning." Hale poked his head through a row of bleachers to look at Shane. "It's an off-day. Wouldn't you rather be at the beach?"

"Maybe later." Shane focused on cleaning, hoping Hale might leave, but Coach just hung around.

"Shane, would you mind coming out from under there?"

He crawled into the sunlight then felt woozy from standing up too quickly. It was the hottest part of the afternoon and Hinton Fields was uninhabited except for the two of them.

"So how are you?" Hale asked.

"Good."

Hale placed his hands on his hips and waited for a real answer.

"I feel dumb about yesterday," Shane said. "I blew it in front of those scouts."

"No one expects you to play perfectly. Those guys are here to see your potential."

"I left my potential at home yesterday."

"Will you quit that? I can have all the confidence in the world in you, but it doesn't matter if you don't feel that way about yourself." Hale held up a hand to shield his eyes from the sun. "Let's go in the shade."

They moved into the shadow of the Rec Center. "You're so close to breaking through to a different level of play," Hale said. "But I can tell there's something you have to tackle first."

Hale formed a fist with his right hand and placed it over his heart.

Shane nodded in agreement.

"Forget about picking up trash. I'll save that for when I need to punish someone."

"Thanks, Coach."

"Go for a swim. That always clears my head."

•　　　•　　　•

Shane entered the house barefoot. The salt water had done him good like Hale said it would. He felt restored as he came into the kitchen, only wearing his blue swimming trunks.

Marie stood by the counter, staring into the steam of her tea.

"Where's Lexi?" Shane asked as he got a glass of water. He chugged it down and turned back to face Marie, who was still looking at her drink. "Mrs. Henson, are you okay?"

"We need to have a talk." She set her mug down and removed Troy's dog tags from her sweatshirt pocket. "I found these at my garden today. Do they belong to you?"

Shane exhaled in relief that the tags had been recovered. Then he saw Marie's disheartened expression when she handed them over.

"That's your brother?"

Shane read MONOGHAN, TROY A. on the tags and flipped them over a few times with his fingers. "Yep."

"Why didn't you tell us he was a soldier?"

"I... I wasn't sure how you would feel..." He could sense his ears going red.

"How I would feel about what?"

"We had that dinner... You said joining the army was... I don't know."

Marie buckled her hands down on the kitchen island, like the room was shifting and the surface might steady her. "Did you leave those tags there on the 4th? When you came to help out?"

"They might have fallen off my neck that day," Shane said. "Or maybe out of my bag."

"So you haven't been to the garden any other time?"

An unwanted flash came to his mind as he saw himself taking a bat to the harmless flowers.

Such easy targets; what a sad excuse for a vandal you are.

He knew Marie wasn't going to be surprised or livid. She had already put the pieces together, but it was important that he said the words aloud. "I destroyed your garden."

"Why?"

"I found out my brother was going back to war. And I got mad..." Shane crossed his arms over his bare chest, wishing he had more clothes on for the conversation. "I was upset. It was stupid –"

"I believe that you didn't do it maliciously," Marie said. "But what doesn't sit right with me is how easy it's been for you to lie the last week."

"What can I do to fix it?"

"I need a few days. Can you stay with one of your teammates while I think things over? Then we can talk and –"

"I'll just figure out another place to stay," Shane said.

"That's not what I'm asking."

"I know. But it's better if I go."

"I didn't say I wanted you gone," Marie said in frustration. "I just need some time to figure this out."

They both kept quiet. Shane scratched at bits of sand in his hair before he put the dog tags around his neck and went up to his room. He pulled the suitcase out from his closet and began packing his clothes. His phone lit up on the nightstand as he received a new text from Troy.

Hey bro. How are things in paradise?

13

"Stag's Pond"

The full moon hung low over the trees of Barber's Woods. Shane stared at it from the Burnsdale neighborhood where he and Lucas hunted for the town's remaining little green dudes. After half an hour of scouting on foot, they spotted a prized figure in front of a ranch-style house.

Lucas made a slow approach up the cement drive that was covered in hopscotch squares and chalk monsters. He tried to snatch the figure but was thrown off by some pullback. "I'll be damned."

"What's wrong?" Shane crouched down as he moved over. There was a bicycle lock fastening the green dude to a post in the front yard.

"I've got my pocketknife," Lucas said.

"It won't cut through."

Lucas pulled his knife out and started to carve.

"Luke, just leave it," Shane said. "Someone will see us."

"What? You think I can't do it?"

"Hey," a guy shouted from the home's doorstep. "What are you doing?"

The outside lights came on. Lucas spun around and locked eyes with the middle-aged man. "Run."

They bolted for the street with the pit-pat of the man's footsteps following behind them. A passing car beeped as Shane and Lucas dodged traffic and entered Barber's Woods. They ran to the bike path that cut through the forest. The trail got dark as a thin sheet of clouds obscured the moon's ghostly glow.

Shane heard a peaceful cluster of notes forming from a wind chime. "Lucas, I think we're in the clear," he said and stopped running.

"Out of all the driveways in the town I had to pick that one." Lucas slowed his pace.

"You know that guy?"

"He's the pastor at my host family's church. And he definitely recognized me."

Shane broke into a heaving laugh that sounded like he was fighting for air. "Good luck with that one."

"I'll say I was bringing my troubled friend over for guidance, but you chickened out."

Shane let out one last joyful sigh and wiped a tear from his eye. "You're gonna lie to preacher-man?"

"Sometimes it's better to lie." Lucas crossed over to a cemetery along the path. "Come on, we can cut through this way."

The graveyard was expansive and contained mossy headstones from the town's first few generations of residents.

"Look at that." Lucas pointed to three eighteen-wheelers parked by the cemetery's front entrance. Adjacent to the vehicles, there were disassembled carnival rides strapped down to trailers. "Must be for the fair," Lucas guessed.

Shane saw the carousel ponies and Ferris wheel carts. "Now that seems like a jinx… to keep all that stuff *here*," he said, gesturing to the plots.

They went to the church parking lot where Lucas left the Corolla. He let the keys idle in the ignition once they were back inside the car.

Shane watched his friend slip into a solemn state. "You about to go confessional on me?"

"Yeah. Remember those scouts at the foggy game last week?" Lucas said. "Well, one of them contacted me about playing for their team."

"That's awesome. Why do you sound so sad?"

"You don't get it. They're not exactly the Yankees. It's some circus league."

"You should still check it out."

"They don't even pay their players."

"But it would be a way to keep baseball in your life and –"

"And it'd be a total embarrassment." Lucas smacked his hands against the wheel then was jarred by the horn honking. "I never thought it would end so shitty."

"Come on, Lucas. You know… It's not like…"

Lucas started the engine. "I'm sorry. I'm blaming the full moon for that Eeyore shit. I'll drop you at the Hensons."

Shane itched the back of his neck. He had yet to tell his friend, or anyone in the Cove League, about leaving his host residence.

Sometimes it's better to lie.

"I stashed my bike on Main Street earlier. You can just drop me there."

Lucas parked the Corolla by the library lawn to let his friend out. Shane walked past big elm trees and a bronze World War II memorial plaque as he approached the bike rack. It was eerie that the tourist town was so quiet on a summer night. No drunks stooped on the sidewalks and no cars passed with pop songs playing too loud.

Shane checked his phone screen, a new voicemail from Coach.

"Hey, Shane. Hale here. I tried to get in touch with Noah's family but I haven't heard back from them. I've got the home address here if you need to stop by and get your glove; it's 134 Dearborn Avenue, which is in Green Banks. Alright, see you tomorrow."

Why'd Noah stop coming to workshops all of a sudden?

Lucas said the kid did the same thing last summer.

Something is off. You should check on him.

He shivered on his way to retrieve Mildred. It was more than just goosebumps from a breeze. He walked on the grass towards his borrowed bike and scratched at his mosquito bites.

It's too late. Find him tomorrow.

•   •   •

Sleep never came, so Shane turned to the coast for entertainment. He watched a cargo ship pass, maybe on its way to Eleanor's Island. His phone vibrated on the wooden floorboards of the Trunk Drive lifeguard shack. He rolled off his makeshift bed of sweatshirts to answer. It was a call from Kev, his friend and teammate from St. Francis. "Kev. What's up?"

"Shane!" Kev shouted. "I miss you, man. Things are so boring in Oregon."

"How was I lucky enough to make your drunk dial list?"

"Not drunk dial. Is there a term for high-dialing?"

"I don't know, Kev. It's pretty late here."

"Shit. I forgot about time zones."

"I wasn't asleep. What's up?"

"Listen, I gotta talk to you about something and there's no easy way to talk about it."

"Okay… What's on your mind?"

"Calloway."

Shane gulped. "What about him?"

"I know… I know he was abusive to you."

Shane's first response was to shut down. He let the silence grow as he focused on the night's forceful waves.

Kev spoke; "Take as much time as you need. I'm sorry to spring it on you."

"I don't even… I never told anyone," Shane said. "How did you know?"

"I saw how far in your head that guy was. And when you left for college he needed a new target."

"What did he do to you?"

"It was like he was obsessed with me. He started showing up in the middle of my classes. He'd pull me out in the hall and tell me something trivial. Or in the locker room, he'd chew me out in front of the guys, say how I blew my load early whenever I was with a girl."

"Jesus, Kev. Look, he never... Did he make a move on you?"

"Yeah. Like six weeks ago. He had me stay longer than everyone else and do these extra drills. Then in the locker room he... He tried to... He touched me."

"I should have said something last year. This never would have happened to you if I had just –"

"Shane, it's alri –"

"No, it's not. I was just so... I didn't know how to –"

"It's okay. I'm okay."

Shane's right hand stung. He saw a splinter from the floorboards stuck in his palm and yanked it out. "So what happened when he... How did you get out of that situation?"

"I just ran off," Kev said. "Then the next morning I went to Guidance."

"You told them what he did?"

"I didn't tell them who it was, but I said somebody in the faculty had made an advance on me and I wanted to know what my options were."

"What did they say?"

"They talked about how serious the allegations were, how it could go to court. Then they wanted me to give them a name."

"Did you?"

"No. I wanted to think shit over. And I didn't know how much I trusted the school. Then boom. Next thing I know... Calloway's dead."

Shane and Kev listened to each other breathing for a while, both of them in need of the intermission.

"Kev, tell me what you're thinking."

"I still don't know if word got back to Calloway somehow. Or if it was all some bizarre coincidence that he had his wreck that same night."

"It wasn't a coincidence," Shane said. "He crashed on purpose. That way he got off the hook. And he died with all his false dignity still in tact."

"It's like he's still toying with us," Kev said.

Shane exhaled hard enough to hear static over the call. "What are we supposed to do with this?"

"I want to come forward. But I don't want to do it alone."

"Come forward? What would be the point? We already got the best possible outcome. He's dead."

"No one's ever going to know who he really was though."

"You want to dig him out of his grave for a trial? I don't get it, Kev."

"Will you promise me you'll give it some thought at least?"

"I can't do this right now. Good night."

Shane ended the call. The sand felt cool against his bare feet as he made his way to the ocean. A swim would cleanse him of his nerves. He reached for his belt buckle then heard laughter from the bike path; a group of college kids staggered towards the secluded beach armed with abrasive voices and a thirty rack. Shane gathered his belongings and left the shoreline.

• • •

He dried off from the shower and tossed the ripe-smelling towel into the pile of laundry in his locker. There was no clean underwear left so he resorted to turning yesterday's pair inside-out. He put his bathing suit on after, rummaged around until he found a shirt, and went upstairs for dinner.

While he waited for the Animal Crackers to dispense from the vending machine, Frank, the janitor of the Rec Center, came out of the Women's bathroom with his custodian cart. The man was in his sixties, bald, and wore tortoise shell glasses.

"Shane? What are you doing here this late?" Frank asked.

"I was… uh, watching some game film… and I lost track of time."

"How'd you even get in here?"

Shane shrugged and reached inside the machine for his snacks.

"You've been here afterhours a lot lately," Frank said. "Why is that?"

"I like it here."

"Bologna. You've been taking extra showers here. All your stuff's here. This ain't a hotel, kid."

"I just need to stay for a couple more days."

Frank pushed his cart back and forth. "You haven't been having any… sleepovers here… with any ladies? Have you?"

"No, sir." Shane coughed up cracker dust.

"Whom do those belong to?" Frank pointed at the dog tags tied around Shane's neck, hanging from a black shoelace.

"My brother. He's army."

Frank sighed. "You can stay a few more nights. I'll have to talk to Hale if it goes past that."

Frank switched off the overheads as he wheeled his cart away, leaving the cold, blue brightness from the soda machines to light up the hall.

Shane went to the Teen Room. It had foosball tables inside and a long window that gave view to Hinton Fields. He got comfortable on a couch and gazed at the empty diamond like it was his nightlight.

When he did get around to closing his eyes, he couldn't stop the slideshow in his mind. He pictured Noah with a black eye, Calloway steering his car into a tree, skeletons riding a Ferris wheel, Frank the janitor under fire in Vietnam.

A vibration from his phone interrupted the feature. He grabbed his cell and read a text from his Mom: *Hey Shane. Everything ok? Haven't heard from you in a while. Love you.*

He composed his response: *Sorry I've been out of touch. Things have been insane. Let's talk soon. Love you.*

●   ●   ●

There were slits of blue poking through the gray sky above the pond. It would be typical weather for Oregon, but on Nailer's Cove it made for a gloomy day. He stood in the center of the circle of little green dudes with a sealed envelope in his hands. He heard someone coming through the trees behind him.

"Hey, Lexi. Over here," Shane called to catch her eye.

She kept her distance, reluctant to venture too deep into the brush. "Hey… Why'd you want to come here?"

Shane saw her raised eyebrows. He hadn't considered his secret pond was an odd place to meet. "I don't know. I just like it here."

She walked closer. "So… what's up?"

"You know about the garden?"

She nodded. "My mom told me."

"Can you forgive me?"

"I'm not the one you should ask," Lexi said.

"I have this letter trying to explain things. Will you give it to Marie?"

"Please don't put me in the middle of this."

"Okay." He slid the letter into his pocket and went over to sit by the edge of the water. "I'm sorry."

"It's fine." Lexi faced the circle of plastic figures. "What's the deal with these guys?"

"Me and Lucas collect them."

"Why?"

"I don't know. It's our thing. We take them from people's lawns and bring them to the swamp. That's what Luke calls it here."

"This place has a name you know," she said. "It's called Stag's Pond."

"Why Stag's?"

"It's sort of local legend. When we were in middle school, the one across the water there, they told it to us."

Shane crossed his legs for story-time. "Will you tell it to me?" He patted the ground as an invitation.

"Fine." She unzipped her windbreaker and laid it over the mud before she sat. "There was this marine biologist, she came over from England to do some research in Burnsdale."

"When was this?" Shane asked.

"I think the nineteen-fifties. She came over on an ocean-liner and started working in one of the labs when she got here. She was married and for some reason her husband ended up coming over on a later boat. I forget if he drowned or if there was some kind of accident, but he died before he got here."

"Shit. Then what happened?"

"The night she found out about his death she came here." Lexi nodded her head at the water. "I think she was planning to kill herself, but they leave that part out of the middle school version."

"Why wouldn't she drown herself in the ocean?" Shane asked.

"I don't know. Maybe she lived closer to this dump."

"Hey, I told you this is my favorite spot."

"There aren't even benches." Lexi gestured at the muddy surroundings.

"That's why it's cool. It's tucked away, no crowds. You can just come and be alone," Shane explained.

"Alone with your plastic green men?"

"Precisely. They're great listeners you know."

"Unlike you."

"Okay. I'll be quiet."

"Well, it's a good thing the scientist came here because when she was at her lowest point she heard something coming out of the woods..."

"Was it a stag?" Shane guessed.

"It was a huge stag." Lexi stretched her arms out to signify the gargantuan length of the antlers.

"Did it talk to her?" Shane asked.

"Not with words." She laughed at his childlike sincerity. "It came over to her and nuzzled her legs until she got off the ground. It wanted her to keep going."

"No way. I don't believe it."

"Why not?"

"Because deer run when they even *smell* humans. I know this guy back in Oregon who has to use this special soap when he hunts because they can pick up our scent."

"Maybe this lady used the same soap," Lexi said. "Anyway, I don't know if the stag was a sign from God, or if it was her husband's spirit.

Or maybe it was an intuitive animal, in the right place, at the right time. But the woman kept going, and not long afterwards she found out she was pregnant with her lost lover's son."

"Is she still alive?"

"I doubt it. But I think the family still lives in town."

"Hold on a second." Shane's phone shook in his pocket. The number was blocked but he still accepted the call. "Hello?"

"Is this Shane Monoghan?" a man's voice asked.

"Yes it is."

"This is Detective Wald from the Burnsdale Police Department."

The garden. Would Marie report it?

"I need you to come over to the station as soon as possible," the detective said. "Are you in Burnsdale?"

"I'm here. What's going on?"

"A friend of yours is at the station."

Did Lucas get busted by the pastor?

"Who's that?" Shane asked.

"Noah Kinton."

"I'll be right there." Shane shoved his phone in his pocket.

He stood from the dirt and saw the hints of blue had vanished from the sky. He peered down at Lexi, her face seemed unfamiliar to him in the emergency. "I'm sorry. I have to go."

Shane left her by the water and bolted through the circle of green dudes. They held out their flags like they marked the start of a race.

CHAPTER FOURTEEN

"Safe"

His breathing was heavy when he rushed into the police station. Shane approached the lobby's lone sentry, an officer with a fresh crew cut who sat in front of a bulletproof glass barrier.

"Is Detective Wald here?" Shane asked.

The cop held up a *gimmie-one-sec* index finger then spoke into his phone's receiver: "What you can do is call that maroon of a delivery boy and tell him to come back with some dressing."

Where's Noah?

Shane scanned the room for another officer to help him, but the only other person there was an elderly woman reading a magazine.

"That's not my problem if he already drove back," the cop said.

"My friend might be in trouble," Shane said.

The man ignored him. Shane gripped a ceramic bowl filled with peppermints and wanted to smash it against the wall.

"Caesar would be great. Thank you." The cop put the receiver down and looked to Shane. "What's up, kid?"

"Are you sure you don't have anything more important to take care of?" Shane pointed to the man's naked chicken salad.

"Easy there, bullseye."

"I need to see Detective Wald."

"What's the name?"

"Shane Monoghan."

"And what are you here to see Detective Wald about?"

"Noah Kinton. I don't know why he's here. The detective didn't tell me on the phone. Do you know if –"

"Take a seat."

"You can't tell me what happened?"

The man with the crew cut offered no reply. He punched numbers into a keypad then went through a padded door and out of sight.

Shane waited beside the older woman wearing big bifocals and a disintegrating straw hat. "My grandson Jeremy is here to file a report," she said.

He noticed the woman was flipping through a copy of the Burnsdale Brigs Summer Guide. "I hope that works out for him," Shane said.

"Why are you here?" she asked, still admiring the idyllic Cove League photos.

"A friend of mine is in trouble."

"Will he be okay?"

"I don't know… I knew he was in a bad spot… but I didn't speak up."

A man with broad shoulders moved behind the opaque glass and entered the lobby. He wore black boots, chinos, and a navy button-up despite the summer heat.

"You're Shane?" Detective Wald's dapper aesthetic and his quaffed hair made him look like an actor playing a cop, but the holstered weapon and silver badge on his belt seemed real enough.

"That's me." Shane hurried over to the man. "Is Noah okay?"

"How do you know him?"

"Is he in trouble?"

"What's your relation to the kid?"

"I play for the Cove League. Noah comes to our workshops."

Wald shot him a skeptical glance, but the woman in the straw hat handed over her Brigs Guide with the page open to Shane's biography and player photo. Shane gave the woman a nod of gratitude, as Wald checked back and forth between Shane and his picture.

"Show me this goofy smile here, then I'll know for sure." Wald closed the book and waved for Shane to follow.

There was a hallway behind the glass barrier where the clicks of keyboard typing and the ripe scent of stale coffee filled the air. Wald brought Shane to an observation space with a one-way mirror inside. They could see Noah sitting in a small room on the other side of the glass. His head was slumped down on a table, uninterested with the Lego set spread out before him.

"Been looking for this?" Wald tossed over a baseball glove. Shane saw his name and cell number scribbled in the leather.

"You're lucky he had that on him," Wald said. "I wouldn't have known how to get in touch."

"I'm glad he had it. Where's his grandmother?"

"She's driving back from Boston now. When I asked the kid if there was anyone else we could call, he took that mitt out of his backpack."

They both observed Noah as he fiddled with the blocks. The collar of his sky-blue polo shirt was wrinkled, with one side popped up and the other folded down. Shane could see scratches and red marks around Noah's neck.

"How much do you know about what's going on at home?" Wald asked.

"I know his mother died. I know his dad is... What happened today?"

"The neighbors called in domestic abuse. Third time this year. The dad was gone by the time one of our guys got there. He found Noah in his room. From his neck, it looks like the father had him in a chokehold. Once it's a pattern like this, usually DSS gets involved." Wald stuck his hands in his pockets and let his head rest against the glass for a moment. "This isn't even my beat anymore but my daughter and Noah are friends from school."

"So what happens now?" Shane asked.

"It's up to the grandmother. I'll talk with her when she gets here."

"Can I take him out for a while?"

"You're not exactly family."

"Call Beatrice. She can vouch for me." Shane watched Wald's eyes wander and knew the detective was entertaining the idea. "We won't go far. That way Noah doesn't have to spend the day sleeping on a Lego set."

"I asked around the station. That was all I could find for him."

"I didn't mean to sound —"

"Let's get Grandma on the phone and see what she says." Wald left the observation room.

The door was slow to close. Once Shane heard it shut, he slipped his hand into his the worn leather of his glove. He placed the mitt against his heart and let out a gentle sigh.

•　　　•　　　•

The café had no air conditioning yet there was still a line of customers stretching out the door. The tourists wore cycling outfits, summer dresses, designer sunglasses, and bright tank tops. Some stared at smartphones while others debated their choices on the beverage menu.

After they received their mixtures of chocolate milk and iced coffee, Shane and Noah found a table that had a chessboard engraved into the wood, along with a complete set of pieces to play with. Noah spent a great deal of time contemplating each move, but he quickly lost his front line of defense. The boy gulped his drink then nudged his final pawn closer to Shane's side. "Your move."

Shane claimed it with a knight. He watched as Noah ventured a rook out into battle, leaving his king open to attack. "That'll cost you."

Noah became incredulous after seeing Shane knock his royalty down. "No fair. You have to say 'check.'"

"Is that how that works?" Shane spotted tears forming in Noah's eyes and his voice became sympathetic. "I was joking. I'll take it back. Don't get upset."

"It's not the game." Noah focused on someone across the café. It was a young father with a sleeping newborn against his chest. The man rocked the baby, shushing it to sleep.

"Hey, I made a different move. It's your turn." Noah used his shirtsleeves to wipe at his eyes.

• • •

Shane stepped under the awning of the station as the drizzle began. Then Noah and his grandmother did the same to avoid getting wet. It was the first time Shane had seen Beatrice for more than a passing moment. She had salt and pepper hair but the same freckles and sharp nose as her grandson.

Noah stuck out an open palm to let the rain hit his skin. "Shane, will you still have your game?"

"I just got a text from Lucas. It's cancelled."

Beatrice tapped Noah on the shoulders. "Go wait in the car."

The boy darted down the stairs and past the row of police cruisers while Beatrice gave Shane a hug. "Thank you so much for looking after Noah 'til I could get here," she said. "He must really feel safe with you. That boy doesn't trust people easily."

"He means a lot to me." Shane stepped out of the hug. "I was worried when he wasn't coming to workshops. I wanted to call."

"His father is so inconsistent, so Noah falls out of his routines. But now it's looking like I'll have to step in," she said. "If my Lyla were here…"

They both watched the parking lot as the patter of the rain got louder.

"I can help out with Noah," Shane said. "If you need it."

Beatrice shook her car keys in the direction of the neighboring Rec Center. "A few days ago I went in the Rec to pay Noah's admission for workshops. I bumped into my friend Frank, the custodian. Your name came up and Frank told me you'd been *sleeping* there. Is that true, Shane?"

"It's just short-term."

"Did something happen with your host family?"

"I did something," he mumbled. "I messed it up."

"Well, I'd still like to invite you to stay with me and Noah. We have an extra room. Noah needs a friend. And honestly, I need some backup." She let out a tired laugh then stuck Detective Wald's card into her wallet. "As far as what happened at the last house, have you made it right with them?"

"Not yet," Shane said.

"Well, we've figured out your end of the deal then. Make amends with them and help me with Noah." Beatrice scanned the parking lot. "Where did he run off to anyway?"

"You told him to go wait in the car."

"I'm not always this scatter-brained." Beatrice said as she braved the rain. "I have your cell number now. I'll call you when your room's ready."

Thunder rumbled on Shane's trek to the Rec Center. Branches flung off trees and power lines swayed in the distance so Shane was shocked to see someone sitting on the bleachers by Hinton Fields. As he got closer, he realized it was Max that was getting soaked. His teammate was indifferent or oblivious of the storm around him. A song called "Do You Remember Walter?" by the Kinks played from his phone.

"Max? What are you doing out here?"

Max cradled a bobblehead toy in his hands.

"I thought it was bad luck for Snoopy to leave your locker," Shane said.

"I had to clear it out."

"Why?"

"Got released from my contract. I leave tomorrow."

"What? Wait. Come tell me over here." Shane brought Max to the cover of the dugout and wiped peanut shells off the bench before they sat. "Why do you have to go?"

"I got called up," Max said.

"This is *good* news?"

Max smiled with poise. "I'm going to the Majors, baby."

"You got called up to the Big Leagues?" Shane hugged Max over his dripping hoodie. "Tell me how it went down."

"L.A. made me an offer back in June but the signing bonus was weak. I figured I'd do one more year of college ball and test the waters again. But they must've changed their minds 'cause they came through with the money."

"I don't get it. Why aren't we celebrating?"

An American flag was flapping in the harsh wind overhead. Max stared at the banner like he was awaiting a similar fate. "It's like you said on the Fourth, '*Mighty Max, Mighty Max, just how long can a hot streak last?*'"

"I was messing around," Shane said.

"But what if I'm hot now, then they drop me the second I cool off?"

"That won't happen. I've seen what you can do. You're gonna knock 'em dead."

"Thanks, man."

Shane listened to the wind howl as Max's music ended. "So why are you out here in the storm?"

"I'm avoiding saying goodbye to Lexi." Max tucked Snoopy in his sweatshirt pocket. "I thought we'd have more time."

"But you gotta go be a star now," Shane said.

"Don't get me wrong. I'm pumped for what's next. But this place... This league... There's nothing else like it. I guess it was too good to last."

They left the dugout. Shane was cautious as he began his ascent up the slick set of bleachers. "Hold up. You won't see the team before you leave. What should I tell them?"

"You'll figure it out," Max said. "Captain."

CHAPTER FIFTEEN

"New Deals"

The Brigs huddled in the Northam outfield that overlooked a harbor of modest yachts and Boston whalers. Shane's hat was stained gray with dirt, tattered after the harsh stomping it received. He struck out three times and was replaying the at-bats in his mind instead of listening to Hale's post-loss analysis.

It had been a week since Max's departure and five consecutive games since the Burnsdale crew had secured a win. All the players were struggling to contribute after the loss of their star. Shane saw Lucas' jersey, soiled from a failed attempt to steal a base. He watched Katzman's occupied eyes, probably calculating how much his ERA shot up during the lackluster outing.

"Anyone else want to talk before we head out?" Hale asked the circle.

"We can't leave it like this," Shane shouted before his teammates dispersed. "We have to kill the jinx."

"Kill the what?" Roman asked.

"The jinx. The bad voodoo. Whatever you want to call it."

"It's not a hex, Shane. It's a rut. And we'll come out of it,"

Katzman said.

"We should have a burn," Shane said.

"Tomorrow. I'm toast." Dennis wriggled out of the huddle.

"You walk away right now and the season is over."

Dennis rejoined the group. "That seems slightly dramatic."

"Listen up, guys." Shane cleared his throat. "I talked with Max before he left and he wanted me to step up... as captain."

"Why are you only saying this now?" Jermaine asked.

"I didn't think things would get this rough. But we clearly work better with a leader. So I'm saying we have a burn."

"You really think it'll break the streak?" Roman asked.

"We have to come together. And it's the best idea I have."

From the corner of his eye, Shane saw Hale standing a few feet away from the huddle. He shook his fist aggressively at Shane, sending the signal to find some grit within and eradicate any remnants of apathy from the team.

"So you guys with me or what?" Shane shouted.

"I like starting fires," Lucas said.

"I'm game," Jermaine said. "Let's cleanse the bad vibes."

"Roman?" Shane tried on a voice full of bravado as he nudged his friend. "You with me?"

"I'm with you," he answered.

"How about you, J.J.? You with me or are you with your phone?"

"I'm with you." J.J. said and shut off his device.

"Allll-riiight!" Shane held the scream like he was belting out the last note of the national anthem. He could feel the chant travel through him, straining his throat, rattling his core, pulsating all the way down to his balls. He pushed against Lucas and Jermaine and watched the ripple spread until the huddle erupted into a mosh pit.

Once the movement simmered, Shane held his left arm up high for silence. "Jermaine, grab any batting lineups and programs from tonight's game. Lucas, try to find that broken bat. J.J, Matt, see that green metal trash barrel?"

"Way ahead of you," J.J. said.

"Coach, can you buy us some time with the bus driver?"

"I'll see what I can do," Hale said.

"I'll break into the shed over there and see if they have gasoline for their lawnmower," Lucas said with widening eyes.

"Dennis, you keep an eye on Lucas. Didn't know he was a secret pyro."

Shane placed his dusty cap back on his head and eased into a smile of disbelief as the Brigs scattered. "Everybody. See that beach by the harbor? Be there in twenty to incinerate all bad vibes."

"What are you gonna do?" Lucas asked.

"I'll get the playlist ready."

•   •   •

The kids on the carousel were enamored of bright lights and toy horses while a nostalgic ballad called "The End of the World" by Skeeter Davis played through the ride's speakers. The surrounding parents pulled out smartphones and tried to take pictures, but their mementos resulted in streaks and blurs.

Shane idled by the ride and remembered when he saw the carnival gear stashed by the graveyard. Just as he had the thought, the merry-go-round came to a jolting stop. The children whined while parents called out for an operator. Shane walked away. When he turned back a moment later, the lights reignited and the mechanical horses resumed their cyclical voyage.

What if you're the jinx?

He went over to the summer fair's central display. With the addition of white lights along its perimeter, the reconstructed Peace Garden made the fairgoers pause. A married couple wearing fanny-packs stood at a nearby placard and read Marie Henson's artist statement aloud so the small crowd could hear.

"Can you believe someone tried to destroy it?" the wife asked.

"I'm flabbergasted. Who would want to destroy something like this?" said the husband.

The garden featured a low bed of purple amethyst and navy hyacinth that juxtaposed against white, night-blooming tuberoses that were elevated like beacons in the dark.

"It's something, isn't it?" said another onlooker, hovering by Shane.

"It's beautiful." Shane saw it was Lexi Henson next to him.

"You're not here for round two, are you?" She laughed at her joke then led Shane to the carnival's activity booths.

"Are you gonna tell Hale?" he asked.

"Don't you think *you* should?"

The frialator smells permeating the air were so strong that Shane had to drop the conversation. "Do you want food?"

They bought hot dogs, fries, and sodas at the concessions stand. Children on spinning teacups passed in circles as Lexi and Shane shared a picnic table.

"The burn was smart," Lexi said. "You guys needed something like that."

"Thanks. We'll see if it gets us a win tomorrow," Shane said. "Have you heard from Max?"

"He texted me when he got out there. I'm not expecting more than that."

"Do you miss him?"

"Yes. And it sucks. But I'm glad we didn't hold back. We didn't treat it like a fling, which is probably why it hurts so much now." She tucked her hair behind her ears and let her hands linger there. "Will the team make it without him?"

"Max knew how to bring out the best in all of us. I'm not sure if I can do that." He consoled himself with the last of the fries.

"To getting ditched." Lexi touched sodas with Shane in a toast.

A few yards away, they could see kids chasing each other around Marie's garden. "I want to find a way to make it up to your family," Shane said.

"Maybe there's a way we can help each other out. How would you feel about me doing a profile on you?"

"I don't know, Lex. Our last interview didn't go so hot."

"I don't mean some hurried, post-game thing. This would be a longer piece, talking about what it's like to grow up in a military family."

Shane grimaced. "I don't want to exploit my story just to get some publicity."

"It won't be a gossip column. It'd be a way to see each other's perspectives. Maybe that's how you get through to my mom. It's a shot anyway."

"Is anyone going to care though? 'Cause I'm not about to get signed to the Majors next week. Maybe in three years."

"I'm not asking you to be Max."

"So what's the angle?"

She sipped the last of her soda and shook the ice around as she considered. "It's about a ball player with a brother in the army," she said. "And there's no room for him to be proud in a town that's rallying around the Peace Garden. He starts the season on the bench but ends up taking his team to the Championship." Lexi flashed him a coy smile. "Isn't that where all this is heading?"

•　　　•　　　•

KEV:
Hey Shane, haven't heard from you.
Now a good time to call?

SHANE:
Sorry I never got back.
Housemates are asleep now so I can't talk.
Text okay?

KEV:
Where do you stand on coming forward?

SHANE:
I don't know.
Not sure if the time is right.

KEV:
Keeping this secret is making me sick.
What are you afraid of?

SHANE:
That going public will ruin my chances of playing for the Majors.

KEV:
They won't think less of you.

SHANE:
They'll think of me as a victim.

KEV:
It takes guts to do what I'm suggesting.
People will see the bravery in it.

SHANE:
Sounds like it was worse for you.
Maybe you should do this on your own?

KEV:
I saw what he put you through.
And if I come clean I don't want to cover for you.
If we speak out, other kids will too.

SHANE:
I've got a career to think about.
I can't afford a scandal this early.
You're free to do whatever, just leave me out of it.

KEV:
Seriously?

SHANE:

I didn't ask to be part of this.

KEV:
So Calloway gets away with it?

SHANE:
He already did.

KEV:
Why didn't you ever tell the school about him?
Why didn't you warn me?

SHANE:
You're like a little brother.
You know you can always reach out.
But I don't want to talk about this again.

KEV:
I get it.
You're still afraid of him.

CHAPTER SIXTEEN

"A Prayer for the Lost"

His stomach grumbled as he smelled the simmering red sauce. Dinner would be soon. He stood in his new room holding the monogrammed cross in his palm and tracing the initials etched into the wood.

L.N.K. Who was she? How did she die?

He discovered the necklace in a dresser drawer when he moved into Beatrice's cottage the week before. Noah must have hid it in the guest room for safekeeping.

Shane put the necklace on and let the cold cross fall against his sternum, just as his phone vibrated with a call from his brother Troy. All he heard was crunchy static when he answered.

"Troy? You there?"

Disconnected. It reminded him of how the calls from Iraq used to get cut short.

He can't be deployed already. There's no way that already happened.

He clung to the cross around his neck and remembered how back in high school he would kneel before bed and pray for Troy's homecoming. But turning to prayer again for his brother's second deployment felt odd. It was like a variation on double jeopardy; he couldn't ask for the same miracle twice. Maybe that was why he trashed Marie's garden. Something had to pay for him living though the same fear again.

A knock came from behind. "Dinner's ready," Noah said, standing in the doorway.

"I'll be there in a minute." Shane waited to turn back until Noah left. He returned the necklace to its drawer and had to jam it shut from the humidity.

Through the window, he watched a swan float down the coastal inlet and past the dock where Noah kept his deceased grandfather's dinghy tied up. He had to squint to see the name of the vessel painted on its side: *Fiona*.

The soft sounds of Debussy became clear as he walked down the hallway. Each night at seven, Beatrice would switch on the classical station. Although she was a retired English teacher, music seemed to be her passion. She still participated in a local choir, checked out new CDs from the library each week, and made sure Noah practiced his instrument.

Shane breathed between bites of pasta supper and studied the interior of his new residence. There were several purple post-it notes taped on the walls and cabinets. They were reminders about Beatrice's appointments, errands to complete, and titles of recommended books. He noticed framed pictures of the Irish countryside hanging from each wall in the living room.

"Was your husband Irish?" Shane asked.

"No," Beatrice said. "His name was Noah Kinton, too, very English name. I'm the one obsessed with the Emerald Isle. Is Monoghan an Irish name?"

"It is. I think it translates to *monk*."

The word got a laugh out of Noah, making him restart his pasta twirling efforts.

"What's so funny?" Shane asked the boy.

"Monks never have sex," Noah said with a grin.

"Don't adolescents make great dinner conversation?" Beatrice said. "Noah picked *To Kill a Mockingbird* for summer reading. How's it coming along, Noah?"

"I've got it covered."

"Covered? I bet you haven't even opened the front cover."

"That's not true."

"Then what's the main character's name?"

"Uh... Mockingbird?" Noah answered.

Shane laughed at the joke but stopped when he received a stern look from Beatrice.

"Don't think I'm letting you off the hook either," she said. "You've been staying here over a week now and you still haven't apologized to your last host family."

Noah smiled at the admonishment and stood from his seat. "May I please be excused? I need to go kill some mockingbirds."

"Hilarious," Beatrice said.

Noah rinsed his plate in the sink. "So what is the main character's name, Grandma?"

"It's..." Beatrice blanked. "I used to teach that book. I can't believe I'm forgetting this."

"Her name's Scout," Shane said as the boy went down the hall.

"Noah's always struggled with reading," Beatrice said. "He has some learning disabilities and Harris, his father, never gave him the resources he needed to deal with them."

"Why not?" Shane asked.

"Harris never wanted to admit anything was wrong. Even when Lyla died, he didn't really deal with it. He worked more and drank more and distanced himself from Noah. Sometimes I think because Noah looks so much like his mother did."

Shane eyed the walls but saw no pictures of Lyla. "I wish I could've met her."

"You two would've gotten along. You're both nocturnal."

"She didn't sleep well either?"

"Never. She was a sleepwalker, too. I'd find her out here at one in the morning folding linens."

Shane smiled. He went to the sink to wash his dishes. "How did you know I'm a night-owl?"

"You have the same circles she had." Beatrice placed her pointer fingers under her eyes. "She said that was her warpaint."

•   •   •

Lucas felt the ache of an impending brain freeze, so he put his milkshake down and examined the press box with a mix of awe and concern. The space looked like a war room with a large map of Nailer's Cove taking up an entire wall. Rosters and stats of the eight Cove League teams were pinned next to their corresponding towns on the chart. There were notes scribbled about players that had left early, guys that had been injured, and updated ERA numbers for all the pitchers. Roman taped an empty playoff bracket next to Shane's map then resumed sipping his strawberry milkshake.

"Why does everyone have a shake but me?" Shane asked.

"I asked you if you wanted one," Lucas said. "You were too busy planning your invasion of Normandy, or whatever it is you're doing up here."

"We've been updating the numbers. Roman figured out as long as we win two games, we're golden."

"You mean after that losing streak we could still make the playoffs?"

"The Canalmen's main slugger went home early," Roman said. "No one knows why he had to go. But they've only made two runs since. As long as they stay in their slump, we stand a chance."

"Sweet." Lucas used his straw to suck against the bottom of the cup, trying to get every last bit of his treat.

"Roman, do we know what pitcher –" Shane stopped, unable to focus with the grating noise from Lucas' straw.

"It's stuffy up here." Roman went to the corner to turn on a fan then jumped back once he plugged it in the wall. "Whoa!"

The screens of the laptops flickered as the hum of machinery swelled, then disappeared.

"Is it safe up here?" Roman asked.

"Safe enough," said Shane. "Do we know what pitcher Lawrence is – "

"I should have bought the large." Lucas kept slurping.

"Enough with the milkshake." Shane smacked the cup out of his friend's hands. "And don't say I owe you another one. That thing was gone."

"Can we talk for a second?" Lucas pulled Shane over by the windows. "Some of the guys are worried you're getting too intense about being captain."

"'*Some of the guys?*'" Shane said skeptically.

"Okay, *I'm* worried about you."

"When we win the championship, you'll thank me for going mental."

"I get it. I do jigsaw puzzles when I want to avoid dealing with something."

"I'm not avoiding anything."

Roman held up Shane's ringing cell phone. "Someone named Kev is calling you."

"Don't answer it." Shane ducked his head out the window. "Dennis. Where were you for batting practice today?"

"I was… um, volunteering," Dennis answered from below. He wore a turquoise bathing suit and had a towel slung over his sunburnt shoulders.

"Volunteering at the beach?"

"Yeah, um, cleanup committee."

"Just get dressed."

"Okay, Mom."

J.J. rushed into the press box waving his smartphone in the air. "Guys, check this out." He had a clip ready to play on the screen. "It's Max. He got his first home run in the Minors."

Roman and Lucas huddled close to watch the video.

"Ain't that something," Lucas spoke over the applause coming from the device. "Shane, don't you want to see?"

"I'll find it later."

"Shane," J.J. said. "Coach wants you to come find him before the game."

"Okay." Shane looked outside and saw Hale's golf cart speeding toward the diamond while the fans filled up the hill.

"We should start the music. People are here." Shane hit the space bar on the interns' laptop and Bruce Springsteen's "Dancing in the Dark" played over the speakers.

"Will you guys rally the troops in right field?" Shane asked. "I'll be there in a minute."

"You got it," Roman said, while Lucas and J.J. saluted behind him.

Shane left the press box and crossed the ballpark as the kids of Spectator's Hill blew bubbles, chased after Frisbees, and played catch with mitts far too big for their hands.

Then he passed Katzman warming up in the bullpen. Jermaine caught the pitcher's curveball then gave Shane a thumbs-up in approval of the song choice.

Three quick beeps came from Hale's golf cart as the Coach signaled the new captain to join him for a conference by the dugout.

"What's up, Coach? J.J. said you wanted to talk."

"I wanted to tell you how proud I am of all the work you're doing," Hale said. "Leading the practices, working on infield communication, it's all very impressive."

"Thank you. That means a lot." Shane got flustered. "I want to get you that big championship trophy."

"That's not what's important to me. You know that. Now go be with your brothers."

"Did Lucas show you the prayer?"

"He did. I think it'll be good for morale." Hale patted Shane on the back and descended into the dugout.

The Brigs gathered in right field for the pre-game huddle and Shane was pushed to the center of the tight circle.

"Shane's gonna say something," Lucas announced to the group.

"Preach." Jermaine nodded at the cross hanging from Shane's neck that had popped out from under his jersey.

"Me and Luke have been talking about ways of keeping the positive vibes going. I'm not particularly religious, and I know we all have different faiths, so I decided to write something –"

"Shane, are you turning this into a cult?" Matt flicked a bumblebee away before it could nest in his beard.

Roman shushed the whole bunch. "Let Shane talk."

A swarm of deodorants filled Shane's nostrils as he blanked on how to start.

Lucas coughed to get his captain's attention then mouthed the first two words to jog Shane's memory.

"Dear Lord." Once Shane spoke the Brigs having side conversations on the outer ranks quit talking. He continued:

"Stop my pants from tearing when I'm stealing second base
Protect my pearly whites when the fastball's by my face
Make my hits soar so the ball never knows an adversary's glove
Keep my brothers safe, bless us Brigs with all your love
Amen"

•　　　•　　　•

He waited on the front porch of the Henson house as a welcome breeze broke the heat. When no one answered the door, he checked his reflection in the glass. He pushed his bangs around and smoothed down the sides of his hair.

His apology to Marie was memorized, but he felt foolish for not bringing a peace offering. He straightened his posture as Lexi opened the door.

"Shane... Bold move showing up here. I like it." She held a paperback behind her, preventing him from seeing the book's cover.

"What are you hiding there?"

"This book I used to read when I was a kid." She revealed a copy of *The Golden Compass* by Philip Pullman.

"I know that book. I liked how they all had the little spirit animals. What do you think yours would be?"

"A sea otter maybe... Wait, why are you here?"

"I wanted to talk to Marie. Is she home?"

The crunch of tires against the driveway made them both look back as a yellow taxi arrived.

"You expecting someone?" Shane asked.

"Not that I know of," Lexi said.

A tall man in his mid-twenties stepped out from the back of the cab. He was dressed in army camouflage and had Timberland boots on his feet. The car pulled away with a farewell honk, leaving the man standing under Fred Henson's withered American flag.

"Do you know him?" Lexi asked.

"That's Troy," Shane said. "My brother."

CHAPTER SEVENTEEN

"Welcome Wanderer"

Shane placed three crumpled dollar bills in the Fishmonger's jukebox and chose a few songs he thought might liven up the place. Lexi picked the dive bar as a location for interviewing the Monoghan brothers, although she was running late. That left Shane a few minutes to tell Troy about the nature of Lexi's article before she arrived at the dingy establishment.

A marine construction crew clad in Carhartt jackets took up most of the space at the bar, with Troy lunging between them to order his drink. Shane intermittently locked eyes with an oafish, orange-haired member of the gang. The man appeared to be snickering at Troy, who had worn his camouflage fatigues for the trip to Nailer's Cove.

The opening chords of Fleet Foxes' "Blue Ridge Mountains" played over the bar's speakers while the hunchbacked bartender with boxy bifocals grinned at the tip Troy left him.

"Our theme song," Troy said to Shane as they returned to their booth in the corner.

There was a mirror along the wall where Shane could see their reflections. They both had their mother's pointed nose, but Troy's ears didn't stick out like Shane's did. Troy's skin was olive and his black hair was cut high and tight. His muscular arms each hosted a tattoo; triquetra on the left, grim reaper on the right.

"Hope you don't mind me springing the visit on you," Troy said.

"Are you kidding? I'm so happy you came."

"Well, you weren't answering my calls."

"I'm sorry. I've been so busy with the league." Out the window, Shane watched while a golden sliver of the sun dipped beneath the ocean. He hadn't considered the pain his silence could cause.

"It's alright. We're together now," Troy said.

"Yeah and you get to see a big game tomorrow."

The men at the bar broke out in muffled laughter, the one with the red beard covered his grin when he met Shane's glance.

You're not inventing it. Ginger Beard is talking about you.

"So how's it going with the Brigs?" Troy said.

"If we don't win tomorrow, then we're done."

"Glad thing I came out here then."

Shane laughed at the term from his childhood. It was first used when he knocked a lamp over playing ball inside the house. Troy caught the fixture before it hit the ground, prompting Shane to say, "Glad thing you saved it." *Glad thing* became Shane's go-to term whenever he had a close call. Troy enjoyed his little brother's invention too much to tell him that *good thing* was the correct expression.

"Yeah, glad thing." Shane drank his soda and eyed Ginger Beard.

"I heard all the pitchers in this league are nasty," Troy said.

"My batting average has never been this low."

"All hail President Putin!" Ginger Beard shouted in a forced Russian accent from the bar and stared straight at the Monoghan brothers.

"Down with the capitalist American pigs," another guy added as the rest broke into giggles, slapping their hands on the counter.

"Do you want to go?" Shane asked.

"No," Troy said, unfazed by the men. "Tell me about the reporter who's coming to meet us. Are you two… an item?"

"No. I mean, I think she's… No. We're not."

"Any particular reason she's interviewing you?"

Shane tapped his fingers along with the music. "Actually… she wants to interview *us.*"

"She wants *my* two cents about baseball?"

"She's probably going to ask you about the war."

Troy gulped his beer. "And you're telling me this now? Five minutes before she shows up?"

"It's okay if you don't want to do it."

"I just got blindsided here. Give me a second." Troy gazed out the window as the nearby drawbridge rose for a houseboat's entrance into the crowded harbor.

"Do you trust her?" Troy asked.

"Lexi? Yeah, she's a pro."

"If we're doing this, I need a stronger drink."

"Well, Well, Well" by John Lennon was the next song up in the queue. Shane noticed his brother's footsteps fall in sync with Ringo Starr's thumping bass drum as he walked to the bar where the buffoons got quiet. He considered the possibility that Troy might have put on an air of calm about the mockery and beneath it he was seething.

Lexi entered the Fishmonger, spotted Shane in the corner, and approached the booth.

"Hey, Lex."

"Thanks for making this happen." She sat across from him and removed her digital recorder from her purse. "Why did your brother think you were still staying with us?"

"Did the interview already start?"

"Seriously. You haven't told your family about the garden either?"

Troy came back clenching three shots of amber liquid. "So you're the reporter?" He set the drinks down on the table and offered a shot to Lexi.

"You get straight to business," she said.

"Shane said the same thing about you." Troy slid a glass across the table to his sibling. "One won't hurt 'ya."

"You guys ready to start?" Lexi asked.

"We should have a safe word," Shane said.

"How about *lavender*?" She smiled and raised her whiskey. "To the Brigs."

•   •   •

LEXI: So technically you guys are half brothers?

SHANE: Same mom, different dads.

TROY: We grew up together. We're just brothers.

LEXI: When did you know Shane was going to have success with baseball?

TROY: Even when he was four, it was all he wanted to do. He'd be out playing with other neighborhood kids all year long. He found his path early.

LEXI: Did you have an equivalent of that when you were young?

TROY: I didn't have plans to enlist when I was a toddler if that's what you mean.

LEXI: What made you want to join the army?

TROY: I tried college first before I went in the military. I studied in Boston but the school wasn't the right fit. I was there for the Marathon bombing. Me and my roommate were by Fenway when it happened, but his whole family was at Copley Square where the explosions were. He just wanted to get a hold of them and he couldn't. They turned out to be fine, but I hated that feeling... like we were helpless. It wasn't something I could sit on.

LEXI: Shane, you were fourteen at this time?

SHANE: That sounds right.

LEXI: How did your life change when you became a member of a military family?

SHANE: I missed Troy. That's for sure.

LEXI: So you guys were close?

SHANE: Troy was the one playing catch with me as a kid. He'd make up drills for me, throw me pitches for hours. I wouldn't be here if it weren't for him.

TROY: Shane got where he is because *he* put in the work.

LEXI: What about Coach Calloway?

TROY: What about him?

LEXI: Did he have anything to do with Shane's success?

TROY: Calloway was a bad coach.

LEXI: Can you elaborate on that?

TROY: He was always projecting his goals onto Shane. Trying to have Shane succeed where he didn't.

SHANE: Why are you asking him about this?

LEXI: 'Cause I want his insight.

TROY: One time Calloway ditched Shane and his friend on the highway. Mom had to drive an hour and pick them up on the side of the road.

LEXI: Why would Calloway do that?

SHANE: It doesn't matter.

LEXI: I think it does.

SHANE: This won't be a very interesting article.

LEXI: Please tell the story.

SHANE: Our high school team, the St. Francis Falcons, had stopped at a Burger King after an away game. We had been there for like half an hour already, and my friend Kev went back in line again, even though Calloway told us it was time to go. Kev wanted to try some cookies & cream milkshake. All the guys on the bus were getting antsy and after five or ten minutes Calloway told the driver to just go. I was like, "Hey, Kev's still inside." So Coach told me to get out. And that me and Kev could walk home together.

LEXI: That's awful.

TROY: Calloway was an awful person. They left that out of the obituary.

SHANE: Can we please talk about something else?

LEXI: Okay. Are you worried about Troy deploying again?

SHANE: I... Uh... I'll worry about him. Of course I will.

TROY: Our Mom's worried about –

GINGER BEARD: Hey, soldier boy. Drop and give me twenty.

SHANE: We don't have to stay here if those guys are bugging you.

TROY: Forget them. We'll leave when we're ready.

LEXI: What were you saying?

TROY: Our Mom's worried about Shane. Which is a nice change of pace for me. She asked me to come out here and check on him.

SHANE: Why are you saying this on record?

TROY: 'Cause it's my job as your older brother to pull this shit. And I guess when you talked to Mom on the phone last you freaked her out.

SHANE: What did I even say to her?

TROY: I don't know but she wanted me to make sure you're okay.

LEXI: So are you?

TROY: Yeah, Shane. Are you?

SHANE: You guys are having way too much fun with this.

GINGER BEARD: What the fuck is this music?

TROY: This is John Lennon, asshole.

GINGER BEARD: Paul McCartney forever.

LEXI: Will you guys shut up?

GINGER BEARD: Go blow, Yoko.

SHANE: Let's just leave.

LEXI: I'm gonna shut the recorder off. I got what I needed.

•   •   •

"I'll see you guys at the game tomorrow." Lexi nudged her way out of the booth while the Lennon song on the speakers collapsed into a tantrum of screams.

Ginger Beard stood from his barstool once Lexi left and postured tall like a lumberjack. "Hey, G.I. Joe. Is this the music you use to torture prisoners?"

Troy downed his beer and left the booth with his empty glass in hand.

"Don't do it," Shane pleaded.

"You don't need to worry about me, Shane."

"It's not you I'm worried about."

"I'm just getting another beer. I promise."

The breeze got cold, so Shane closed the window. He watched the drawbridge slowly retract before he heard a jarring thud. His first guess was a mechanism in the bridge must have broke, but Shane realized where the noise had come from when he faced his brother. Troy's constricted fingers held Ginger Beard's head against the bar. Then the man was used as a projectile to knock all his cronies down in a pile of barstools and spilled drinks.

"What are you doing?" Shane asked after the sudden attack.

"Settling up," Troy said. He reached in his pocket and threw a twenty down for the shocked bartender.

"I'm still calling the police," the old man said after snatching the money.

"Time to go, Shane."

The other patrons watched in silence as Shane tiptoed over the men who were either incapacitated or had no desire to face Troy.

Devil's Foot was buzzing outside as the last hints of daylight dissipated. The couples leaving restaurants and the tourists snapping photographs all turned to watch Shane and Troy sprint on the sidewalk and over the lowered drawbridge.

Then sirens started wailing. A police car came down the street and the old geezer from the Fishmonger pointed the cops toward Shane and Troy.

"Just keep moving," Troy said as he led Shane down an alleyway of garbage cans and compost buckets. The narrow path brought them to a residential neighborhood. They hurdled over fences and ran through front yards, dodging tricycles and lawn gnomes. Then Troy stopped when they reached a chapel. It was a small structure surrounded by elm trees with a crumbling statue of Mother Mary. She gestured the brothers to come forth.

Troy rushed to the side of the chapel, pushing hard against a door only to discover it was locked. He waved Shane to follow him behind the building where they went down a back staircase. Troy tried the basement door but it didn't budge.

"People can talk as much shit about me as they want," Troy whispered. "But those guys started making fun of Lexi." He knelt in the alcove.

"I get it." Shane sat beside his brother. "We can hide out here for a bit."

Troy pulled out a canister of chewing tobacco and prepped himself a dose. "You ever do dip, Shane?"

"Not really."

"It helped me stay up in the desert when I had to drive all night." Troy placed the wad in between his lower gums and his teeth. "I used to hide it from you, but... I've done worse things than this."

Shane stared at the bulge in his brother's cheek where the chew tobacco sat. "I got kicked out of Lexi's house," he said. "Her mom's a landscape designer and I destroyed one of her gardens."

"Why'd you do that?"

"I was mad at you."

Troy spit into a pile of dead leaves. "I should tell you... I got my orders."

"When are you leaving?"

"End of August."

"Iraq again?"

Troy nodded. "I get it if you're mad."

"I just don't want you to go." Tears welled up in Shane's eyes.

"Come here." Troy wrapped his brother in a hug. "I'll be okay over there. I'll make it home again."

"Yeah, but what keeps you from going back a third time? When will it end?"

"You're too old for me to lie to you." Troy pulled back. "I don't think it ever ends."

CHAPTER EIGHTEEN

"Wildball"

His pace was sluggish as he moved closer to the melody. The notes became clear once he arrived at Noah's room, where the boy sat cross-legged on his bed, playing a Casio keyboard. Hockey posters and nautical maps of Nailer's Cove decorated the walls of the messy space. Shane stood by a purring fan and listened to the boy's song.

"Always fall asleep with the TV on
Your dreams get funded by telethons
Coca Cola bottles for target practice
Gotta make it home for pancake breakfast
Give us a frown
Like we're saving a stray
Hope you did your stretches
For these big brother days
A ghost on your shoulder
A hero down the hall
Catch it if you can
The wildball
You're as tall as the floodlights

When the crowds all call
But don't spend your life chasing
A wildball"

Noah shut his mouth once he noticed Shane in the doorway, but continued playing the chord progression.

"I've never heard of a wildball," Shane said. "What is it? A kind of pitch? A new sport?"

"It doesn't exist yet," Noah answered. "That's why it's cool."

"Did you write that?"

"Yeah, but I think I lifted the melody from another song."

Shane went to a swivel chair and rearranged some beach towels and bathing suits so he could sit. "Do you take piano lessons?"

"I use online tutoralls... Ah. I can't say that word. Tu-tor-i-als. And sometimes I figure things out by ear."

"I'm impressed."

Noah hit a sour note and winced. "You think you'll chaperone for the Cooperstown field trip? My Grandma can use her Social Security to pay for me."

"It'd be cool, but that'll be after I go back home," Shane said.

"I thought you were staying here now."

"Not forever. I have to go back to Oregon, get ready for the fall semester, spend some time with my family..."

Noah lingered on a moody chord that left his progression unresolved.

"But we won tonight though," Shane said. "Which means I might be around for two more weeks, depending on how far we take it in the playoffs."

"You guys will win," Noah said like a bored prophet. He plugged a pair of headphones into his keyboard, letting Shane know he was done having an audience.

Shane walked to the kitchen where a hanging lamp fixture's orange light filled the room. When he put the kettle on for tea, he saw the post-its that served as Beatrice's reminders. Some of the notes had duplicates or triplicates on the cabinets. There were three that read *Give Noah Check for Cooperstown* and two *Movies with Joanne Sunday.*

He found the copies odd but went back to preparing his drink.

Beatrice came in the kitchen wearing a bathrobe over her pajamas and holding a stack of photographs. "Should I get the couch ready for Troy again?"

"No. He caught a bus after the game tonight. It was a short visit."

"I'm glad we got to meet him." Beatrice sat at the kitchen table and cleared aside the newspapers and magazines. "Have a seat with me. I want to show you something."

Shane joined her and saw the pile of photos she had. The top one was of a freckle-faced toddler standing near the edge of a lake. "Is that Noah?"

"Doesn't he look the same?" They flipped through the album together. "I was looking for my sewing kit today 'cause I saw you had a tear in your jersey. I found these stashed away instead."

"How old is Noah here?"

"Two, three maybe. His parents used to take him up to a lake in the Berkshires when he was little."

In the images, Noah rode on top of his father's broad shoulders, he fiddled with the straps of an oversized life vest, and was snuggled by an attractive woman with milky skin and black hair.

"That was your daughter?" Shane asked.

"That was Lyla... Beautiful Lyla." She displayed the next picture of a luminous Ferris wheel. "There's an amusement park one town over. Noah was probably too young to go on any of the rides."

"You should hang some of these up around the house."

"Noah wouldn't like it. This is the lake where Lyla drowned."

They flipped through the stack together once more but Shane worried when Beatrice started in on a third cycle. The whistling kettle pierced the silence, so Shane went to the range and turned off the front burner.

"Look at the lights on this ride," Beatrice said. "There was this amusement park close to where they used to stay."

"Those are great pictures." Shane focused on his tea. He placed a bag of lemon ginger in his mug and poured the water. Its color changed from soothing gold to murky amber as Beatrice went through the photos once more.

Does she know she already looked at the pictures three times?

Or that she's making copies of all her post-its?

Noah must know she's slipping. That's why he wants me to stay.

A thunderous bang came from outside. Someone's fist had slammed against the house. The sound made Shane drop a bear-shaped honey container and spill his tea.

"What in God's name was that?" Beatrice said.

Shane ignored the puddle of hot water and followed Beatrice into the living room.

She peeked through the blinds. "Oh no."

"What's wrong?"

"Harris is here."

She stepped aside so Shane could see the pale-skinned man who was unrecognizable from the healthy father in the photographs.

"Noah's dad?"

Beatrice nodded then locked the deadbolt.

"Open up," Harris said. He clawed his way out of a beat-up leather jacket and whipped it against the house. His face was gaunt and his hair had patches of white strewn throughout. "Bea, I know you're there. Is Noah up?"

She opened the window to speak. "You want him to see you this way?"

"He needs to see his father."

"Come back when you're sober."

Harris grunted through his teeth and lunged towards the home. The mesh of the screen door was easy for him to destroy. He failed to break through the main entrance, so he resorted to repeatedly banging the doorknocker.

Shane shut the living room window. "You want me to call the cops?"

"The neighbors will if he doesn't shut up," Beatrice said as the ding-dongs of the doorbell began to accompany the obsessive knocking. "Noah doesn't need this nonsense."

Shane pointed to his ears. "I think he has his music in."

They held their positions until the clamor ended. Beatrice stared from behind the blinds and saw Harris sitting on the front steps, his head limp and resting on his knees. "I'm going out there."

"Is that safe?"

"I can handle him." She undid the lock and stepped out.

Shane hurried to Noah's room and saw the boy was still plugged into his instrument, headphones on, rocking his head as he settled into a groove. He let Noah stay in his song.

Shane returned to the living room right as Beatrice came inside. "Where's Harris?"

"Sitting by the water out back," she said. "He told me he was at a bar around here and the staff took his car keys. I have to drive him home now."

"Let him walk."

"He won't make it home in his condition."

"I can drive him."

"Shane, it's not your responsibility."

"But you should be here for Noah."

•   •   •

Shane picked up an aluminum bat from the yard. The youth-sized slugger belonged to Noah and had a tangerine and black design that reminded him of Halloween. There was no moon to be seen in the sky, but Shane spotted red lights on the radio towers in their endless cycle of glistening and fading as he rounded the side of the house. He made it to the backyard and saw a weary figure's silhouette crouching on the dock. The brook that ran through the neighborhood was still, as if Harris' presence had paralyzed the currents. Shane debated if he should drop the bat before Harris noticed, but the man spun around when he realized he was not alone.

"Who are you?" he asked.

"I'm your ride," Shane said.

"You're the ball player..." He pointed to the object in Shane's hand. "You gonna take a swing?"

"I wasn't sure if you had calmed down yet."

"Me? Calm? I'm a pacifist." Harris laughed.

"A pacifist that beats his kid?"

The growl that came from Harris sounded feral and strained. He charged Shane and maneuvered him into a chokehold. Shane dropped the bat as the pressure made his head numb. He writhed in hopes of breaking free. Then the necklace came out from under his shirt, the cross landing on Harris' arm. They both stopped to read the three little letters.

"Why do you have her necklace?" The sight of the heirloom caused his eyes to water. Harris released his grip and collapsed to the grass.

Shane coughed to clear his windpipe and remained motionless until his brain no longer felt like a deflating balloon. Once he had his balance back, he collected his scattered breaths and retrieved the aluminum bat.

"Did Noah give you that necklace?" Harris asked, putting his hands together in beggar's pose. "You two are friends. He'll listen to you. Tell him I just need to talk. Please, will you bring him out here? He needs to know… I didn't mean to hurt him."

"But you did hurt him." A coldness came over Shane as he twirled the bat in his hand. He let it rest by the man's shoulders and looked to the red lights in the sky again like he wanted their permission.

"Don't!" Noah yelled from the house.

Shane turned and saw the boy was watching from his bedroom window. Harris went to wave at his son, but Noah stepped out of sight.

A rush of nausea hit Shane. He tossed the bat into the yard and lifted Harris from his knees. "Come on. Let's get you home."

CHAPTER NINETEEN

"The Towers"

He buttoned up the white jersey before checking his reflection in the bathroom mirror. His face was smooth from a shave, besides a couple strays along his chin. Since he was alone in the house, he was unhurried in preparing for the first playoff game. Beatrice was at the movies with a friend and Noah had left on his bike hours ago for a day of adventuring.

Shane enjoyed the time to himself, but he needed to leave soon. He had to ride Mildred to the Rec so he could catch the bus to Nauset. The Admirals had home field advantage for this matchup and Shane worried it would force the Brigs to lose momentum. Nerves kicked in as he realized he had lost track of time.

"Grandma!" a child screamed from outside the house.

"The hell was that?" Shane stepped over to the window to investigate.

The voice was similar to Noah's but a sense of urgency changed its usual innocent timbre. Shane saw Noah through the window as he stormed into the front yard. The kid clutched his right hand, which was stained red with blood. He howled for his grandmother again.

Shane felt the hair on his arms rise, the beat of his heart race. He launched himself out of the bathroom and knocked over a framed Irish countryside photo on his way out.

Noah paced in circles around the driveway, his hands raised over his head like he was performing some frantic ritual.

"What happened?" Shane said as he went to grab the affected hand.

"Don't touch it. Where's my grandma?"

"She's not here. What happened to you?"

"I was climbing a fence and I cut my hand. And I fell on it."

"How high up were you?"

"I don't know. High!"

Shane saw the blood traveling down Noah's arm and towards his elbow. "You need to let me see it."

Noah's lips protruded in a skeptical frown. He lowered his hands and slowly revealed the right one to Shane. There was a deep gash splitting open his palm. "You think I'll need stitches?"

"You might need a new hand, kiddo."

"What?"

"Sorry. Bad joke. We need to stop the bleeding."

"Can you take me to the hospital?"

Shane ran back in the house without giving an answer. He yanked a thin towel out of the linen closet and tore it into small strips.

"What else? What else?" he asked himself. "Call Beatrice."

Back in the guest room, he found his phone and called her but it went straight to voicemail.

Silence your cell phone before the feature begins.

His mitt rested on the dresser and it reminded him of the fast-approaching game. He picked it up with his free hand. The feel of the leather was a momentary comfort in the chaos.

If you call an ambulance he'll have to go to the hospital alone.

If you take him, you'll miss the bus to Nauset.

"Why are you so slow at everything?" Noah yelled from outside.

"One second." Shane placed his glove down on the dresser.

• • •

The traffic light switched from yellow to red as they neared the intersection. Shane hit the brakes then scanned through the fuzz on the radio.

She only has it on all the time. You think you could remember the station number.

"Will you just shut it off?" Noah said from the back seat.

"Just wait." Shane heard strings and knew he had found the classical station. "This will calm you down."

"I can't calm down!"

"Noah, listen –"

"The light's green."

"Listen to me." Shane accelerated. "Breathe in through your nose and out through your mouth. Like we did in workshops."

"I can't." Noah cradled his injured hand like a broken wing.

"Just do it with me. Okay? In through your nose... And out through your mouth." They did a set together while Shane navigated the car toward the hospital. There were signs in front of restaurants and businesses advertising the start of the playoffs: *Go Brigs!*

Shane placed his fingers on the volume knob and turned down the sorrowful string piece. "Can you tell me what happened now?"

"I was riding my bike back from Green Banks," Noah said.

"What were you doing out there? I thought you were going to hang out with your friends today."

"I went to see my dad."

"Are you serious? Did he –"

"No. He didn't do anything. He wasn't even there.... I did this on my own. I wanted to climb one of the towers."

"What gave you that bright idea?" He saw Noah shut down in the back seat.

Shane turned the vehicle into the entrance of Burnsdale Hospital. "I'm sorry I snapped. I never should have told you about those towers... Is that why you went there? Because of the red fog?"

"What are you talking about? Red fog?"

"Forget it. I thought I told you... What happened when you went to the towers?"

"There's this fence to keep people out," Noah said. "I tried to climb up but there was barbed wire at the top. I didn't realize until after I grabbed it. Then I fell."

"And you used your hand to break the fall?" Shane pulled into a parking space as the classical piece came to its conclusion. The announcer spoke after a brief pause: "That was Dvorak's Nocturne Opus 40, 'The Water Goblin.'"

"What's a water goblin?" Noah asked.

"We'll look it up later."

•　　　•　　　•

Shane and Noah watched a detective show on the overhead TV. The tourist town's ER was packed so they had waited one hour in the lobby before Noah was admitted to the sterile room. Another hour went by before a nurse did the intake.

"Don't be alarmed by the patient across the hall," she had warned them. "She makes noises."

Noah and Shane tried to focus on the show, but the pained groans from the other patient were too bizarre to ignore. A privacy curtain hid the woman from their sight, so Noah grew distressed as he imagined the monster that was close-by and hungry. Shane mimicked the fragmented movements of a zombie to accompany the sound effects.

"Stop it," Noah said with a laugh. "She'll see your shadow."

"Guess we know what a water goblin is now."

Shane felt his cell phone shake in his pocket. He checked and saw another missed call from Lucas.

"You're missing your game 'cause of me," Noah said.

"This is bigger than a game." Shane put the phone away. "I do have to ask you though... You didn't want to climb the towers to... Were you planning on hurting yourself?"

"No. I just needed some space and there was nowhere else to go."

"Is that why you were at Stag's Pond back in June? To be alone?"

"I never told you the stag story. How do you know that's my

pond?"

"Huh? What do you mean it's *your* pond?"

"My great-grandmother, Fiona, she's the woman the story is about."

"No shit." Shane connected the dots; the tale Lexi told him about the scientist who lost her husband, the name of the boat in Beatrice's backyard.

"The night you found me there, it was the anniversary of when my mom died," Noah said. "It's always a bad day for my dad so I took off. I wanted to be somewhere..." the boy trailed as the growling across the hall subsided.

"So what happened when you went to your dad's today?" Shane asked.

"Some random lady answered the door. She said she was the new tenant and that my dad had moved to a town like two hours away from here."

"I'm sorry, Noah."

"I know you don't care he's gone... I saw you that night in the yard."

"I wasn't... That was... I don't know what happened. After he charged me, something else took over."

"Were you going to hit him?" Noah glared as he asked the question, but Shane avoided the eye contact.

"I don't know."

"Then you're just as bad as he is," Noah said under his breath.

The silence that followed ended when Beatrice came in the room. "Noah." She went straight to her grandson's side and gave him a hug. "Are you alright? What happened? Do they know if it's broken? Have you had an X-ray yet?"

"Not yet," Shane said, getting up from his chair.

"Well, what's taking them so long?" Beatrice adjusted Noah's pillows and fixed his posture. The boy was relieved by her presence and enjoyed the pampering, although he hoped Shane couldn't tell.

"I'm so sorry, Shane," Beatrice said. "My phone was on silent because we were in the movies and I didn't see your calls. Thank you for bringing him."

"I hope it's alright I took your car."

"I'm glad it was there. Do you need to go?"

"I should try to catch the end of my game. Can I use your car again?"

"Of course. My friend Joanne is here. She'll give us a ride home." Beatrice patted Noah's hair.

"I'll see you guys at the house." Shane pulled the curtain aside then turned to wave goodbye.

"Hold on, Shane. Don't go. What I said a minute ago... I didn't mean..." Noah faced the window once words failed him.

"I know. Hang in there, amigo." Shane let the screen fall behind him and ran down the hospital's halls.

●　　　●　　　●

The field at Nauset high was crowded with fans of the Brigs and the Admirals. It was the bottom of the ninth when Shane arrived. Though the Brigs were up 4 to 2, the Admirals were staging a comeback with two baserunners on and only one out against them.

Shane pushed through families in the stands. "I think he is late," a little girl told her father as Shane passed.

Gus-the-batboy showered Shane with a handful of Big League Chew.

"What the hell, Gus? Clean that up."

The kid ran off without obeying Shane's orders.

"We can't see," an old man cawed from behind.

Shane realized it was Roman's host-grandparents that were scolding him. The Millers usually greeted him like he was the mayor. Instead, they scowled and waved their arms like air traffic control to shoe him away. The whole ballpark seemed to be aware of his absence.

"Oh, hey Captain Shane," Robbie Cummings said from the bullpen. "Don't worry. You didn't miss much. Not like this is a huge game."

Shane moved toward the visiting team dugout and spotted the sheen of Hale's white sneakers. His coach sat at the edge of the bench with his right hand extended across his face.

"Coach," Shane said to announce his presence.

Hale focused on the diamond. All the guys in the dugout followed suit.

"Just get out of here," Hale mumbled through his fingers.

"It was an emergency. I promise."

"You don't get to pick when you're the captain. These guys were counting on you tonight and you weren't here. Maybe you've got a good reason for missing this, maybe you don't, but your teammates still have half an inning to go. They need to see this through and right now all you are is a distraction."

Shane departed from the field as a collective sigh of relief came from the Brigs fans. The infielders must have turned a double play to save the game. On his walk out of the ballpark, he noticed little red specks scattered across his jersey as the marks of Noah's dried blood revealed themselves under the floodlights.

CHAPTER TWENTY

"Sidelined"

Framed photos of Brigs teams hung on the walls of Hale's office. Shane studied the faces, trying to spot guys that went on to the Majors. He wondered how many of them were ever called in here for a disciplinary meeting.

"Have you booked your ticket back to Oregon yet?" Hale said from behind his desk.

"Not yet," Shane said. "What's going on? Did you talk to Beatrice?"

"I did. She told me about Noah's injury. It sounded like a crazy night."

"So you get why I had to miss the game?"

"Let's talk about the Hensons. How's your stay been?"

Shane bit down on his lower lip and ducked his head.

"Why didn't you tell me you needed to change residences?" Hale asked.

"I wanted to work it out on my own," Shane muttered, keeping his face down.

"I don't understand. Why did you want to leave? Did something happen with Lexi?"

"No. Lexi's great. It was… Do you know the Peace Garden Marie Henson designed? The one that got ruined?"

Hale pushed his chair back against the wall and stayed quiet while he processed.

"Coach…?"

Hale searched for a piece of chocolate in his trail mix then tossed the bag of nuts and raisins into the wastebasket. "Jesus, Shane. You could have been arrested for that."

"I've tried to apologize."

"Sometimes the damage is already done." Hale shifted his focus to the computer screen, his signal for Shane to leave.

"Are you kicking me off the team?"

"It's a privilege to compete in this league," Hale said. "You might lose that privilege."

"Who's going to decide that?"

"Your team will."

"I'm coming to the game tonight," Shane said, trying to restore some command to his voice.

"Don't expect to play."

Shane left the office and wandered down an unfamiliar hallway of the Rec Center. He used an emergency exit by mistake, oblivious to the low hum of the alarm he triggered in his daze.

●   ●   ●

Robbie Cummings whipped his first pitch from the mound to begin the second playoff match between the Brigs and the Admirals. Sports reporters took notes in the press section while photographers aimed their cameras through the fencing. The park regulars watched attentively on Spectator's Hill, the stakes of a possible championship adding a new layer of excitement.

Shane stood in the middle of the crowd with raffle tickets in one hand and a donation jar in the other. He had to stay in the game somehow.

A vibration against his thigh surprised him. The text was from Kev: *Can we talk tonight?*

He sighed at the thought of their last exchange and knew his former teammate might be hounding him about Calloway again.

I have a game right now. You free in a few hours?

The Admirals bats were hot from the start and Cummings loaded the bases minutes into the first inning. All Shane could do was look on as his adversaries began stacking up runs.

•   •   •

His teammates gathered in the outfield after the blowout loss. Their discussion was still ongoing even after Shane helped the interns dismantle tents and run drag mats over the diamond. When the young volunteers left, Shane jogged over to the press box to see Lexi. "Going home?" he asked as he watched her pack up camera equipment from the other side of the fence.

"I can't wait around all night," she said. "Why are you still here?"

"Waiting to see if I get voted off the island." He leaned into the chain-link fence.

"Will it break you?"

"That was a brutal way of phrasing that question."

"Sorry. It's my job."

"No, I'm sorry. This is a rotten ending for your article."

"This isn't the end." She placed her hands on the fence and let her fingers cover Shane's. "No matter what they decide out there."

A charge came over him as he felt her tender skin. They locked eyes as the fuzzy words from the outfield faded and their fragmented breaths crashed like breakers in a storm. Lexi pulled away when Shane stepped closer to the fence. She left him grasping metal as she hurried off with her gear.

•   •   •

Lucas doubted how much longer he could keep the conversation going. Most of the Brigs wanted to send Shane packing when the talk started. He had to remind them not to take their anger from the loss out on Shane. Then he forced the quieter guys to speak, balancing out the stronger personalities. He could feel the energy draining from the huddle as his friends slouched and yawned. It was like an extra innings game. Lucas knew if he endured long enough he could win from the pure exhaustion of his opponent.

"I know he messed up, Coach" Lucas said. "But what you're suggesting sounds like mutiny."

"Anybody else want to throw their two cents in?" Hale asked the group.

Katzman was tight-lipped. Robbie Cummings just spat in response.

"This is your last chance, guys," Hale said. "Do you want to contribute, J.J.?"

J.J. crouched behind some of the other guys' legs for cover as he tried to hide his phone call. "Don't be mad, baby. I'll be there in ten minutes. No, don't give up the table."

"Where is J.J.?" Hale asked.

"I was just stretching." J.J. shot up and kept his phone behind his back. "I'm neutral about Shane."

"I think it's pretty bad he was a no-show for a playoff game." Matt blew a bubble with his gum. It popped and pink fragments got caught in his beard. "Damn it."

"Yeah, so he could take a kid to the ER," Lucas said. "It wasn't like he fell asleep at the beach."

"I still showed up on time when that happened though," Dennis said from the outer ring of the circle.

Jermaine cleared his throat. "I don't know about the rest of you, but I felt like an idiot waiting for Shane to show up and lead that huddle last night. I'm still not sure how we won that game. He doesn't have to go home, but I don't know if he's fit to lead."

"If we let him back then he bails on us again, we'll look like a bunch of chumps," Dennis added.

"Did you forget how we got here?" Lucas said. "The only reason we're even in the playoffs is because that kid rallied us when we needed someone to."

"Exactly," Jermaine said. "He made us all believe in this team. Then he made it seem like it was nothing."

•   •   •

Shane was in the press box, reclining on a beat-up couch. He had grown tired waiting in the dugout and knew the ancient sofa was the only place to get comfortable. He closed his eyes and considered that the agony of limbo might be part of the punishment his teammates had settled on.

The lights flickered. Shane sat up when he heard someone heading upstairs. It was Coach Hale that entered.

"The situation has changed." Hale sat at the intern table. "Your teammates just saved you."

"What do you mean?"

"They all threatened to sit out tomorrow's game if you weren't allowed to finish the season."

Shane rose from the couch and looked out the press box windows. He watched the Brigs walk off the field. It was strange to him that the impenetrable group from eight weeks ago was the same one that just fought to keep him in the game. "So I can stay?"

"Yes," Hale said. "But I want you to know I called Coach Eltman at Goslyn State and filled him in on your summer here."

"Oh." Shane returned to the sofa. "What did you tell him?"

"I told him that you seem unstable. That you've been resisting help. Lashing out in destructive ways. You've been dishonest at times."

"Some progress report."

"I wouldn't be doing you any favors if I let this go unchecked."

"I get it." Shane eased back onto the pillows as if an analysis session was about to start. "Coach, I'm sorry I didn't come to you for help before."

"That's funny. I wanted to apologize to you," Hale said. "You've been struggling and maybe I haven't been a good resource."

"You've been awesome." Shane gazed out the window, seeing quick crackles of orange that illuminated the night sky before they disappeared. "What was that?"

"Heat lightning."

They watched the phenomenon for a while and Shane began to drift. He toyed with the idea of biking to Beatrice's house, but it would take too much time and energy. "Do you care if I sleep up here tonight?"

"I can give you a ride," Hale offered.

"It's peaceful here though."

"Your call, Shane." After a long sigh, Hale rose from his chair and exited the press box.

Shane sent a text to Beatrice to let her know not to expect him then chucked his phone to the floor. The device vibrated in extended bursts once his head fell to the firm pillow. Someone was calling, but Shane had no strength to keep his eyes open.

CHAPTER TWENTY-ONE

"Walk in Darkness"

Shane stood at the diamond's center, staring upwards as night fell over the vacant ballpark. He questioned why the sky was reddening as a warm hand slipped into his shaking one. It was Lexi by his side. She kissed him for a long while with lips tasting like peppermint.

"When there's fire on the diamond, that's when he'll come," she warned.

"Who?"

Lexi knocked on Shane's helmet. It had antlers attached to its sides. "Use your head. You'll know."

She vanished.

"Incredible woman. Truly, an incredible woman," a familiar voice commented. "Down here."

In the dirt, Shane found a baseball card placed in the center of the pitcher's mound. He picked up the laminated Rookie Card for Max DeMello.

"Shane, go back home," Max said, stuck in an akimbo stance on the card.

"Huh?"

"I got this new knuckleball, man." Max appeared before him on the mound and snatched the card away from Shane.

"You're not a pitcher."

"Always thinking in the box. Will you please go home?" Max pointed to home plate.

Shane did as he was instructed. The air was cold. His antler helmet had a cage like a catcher's mask and he lowered it to protect his face. A batter was next to him, but the man seemed frozen. Shane saw it was Lucas, though his skin was neon green. He held a flag out and his jersey had the word SLOW written on it.

"I hope this kid's ready," Max shouted.

The cage kept Shane from speaking so Max's knuckleball knocked the little green dude to the ground.

Jermaine ran on the warning track with his headphones on, giving Shane a hand signal that it was safe to come near. The two switched headgear and Shane heard a song that was familiar yet foreign all at once. Like the girl on the 4th of July who painted his face and made him shiver when she touched his leg.

She was just here. What was she trying to tell me?

He tried to remember what he was trying to remember. Then he saw Noah playing an upright piano by the visiting team's dugout. The boy gave Shane a knowing head nod as he continued the music from moments before.

"What about your hand?" Shane asked. "Isn't it hurt?"

"You must play through the pain," Noah said like a virtuoso. "Your brother is behind you." Noah tilted his head to the stands.

In the distance, he could see Troy was wearing a Brigs uniform as he ran from the bleachers to the Dip Corner where some of the guys chewed tobacco.

Shane was on the track, racing to catch up. Paint dripped from his face and the crowd tossed cheeseburgers at him.

"Liar!" they chanted.

A telephone rang, so he stopped short at the edge of the Rec. He had to run back to the dugout, where the whole team sat on the bench while a landline went unanswered.

"Shouldn't someone get that?" Shane asked.

He moved past the silent crew and towards the receiver but the ringing ceased.

"We missed it," Shane said to the empty bench.

When he woke up in the press box, he heard music coming from the laptop on the table. A song called "The Magician" by Andy Shauf had crept its way into his subconscious, though he swore there had been no music playing when he fell asleep the night before. He tried to recall fragments of the dream, but the harder he worked at retrieving the images the more nebulous they became.

The pops of muscles tearing accompanied his struggle to get off the couch. He wiped dust from his eyes and drool from his cheeks. A gray dawn greeted him when he walked onto the field.

•   •   •

It was still early when he returned to Beatrice's neighborhood. A soft glow came from the cottage's front windows as Shane rested his bike against the fence. Inside, he found Noah channel surfing in the dark. "What are you doing up so early?"

"Couldn't sleep," Noah said.

Shane plopped himself down on the couch and noticed the circles forming under the boy's eyes. "What'd you do last night?"

"I went riding with a friend. There's this bike trail that cuts through Barber's Woods. Then me and Beatrice played Team Solitaire."

Shane smiled at the contradictory name of the game. "Can we go riding on that trail tomorrow?"

"For sure," Noah said. "Hey, did you guys win last night?"

"We lost. I didn't even play. But if we win today –"

"Then you get to stay," Noah finished the thought.

Shane held up crossed fingers and Noah mimicked the gesture, though his hand was still in a brace from the break he suffered a few days before. The next channel featured kids on a baseball diamond in awe of a fireworks display.

"Stop here," Shane said. "It's *The Sandlot*." He grabbed the remote to increase the volume then felt a paper stuck on the device. It was a purple post-it: *Send Electric Bill*.

Shane showed the note to Noah. "Has Beatrice been forgetting things?"

The boy gave a reluctant nod of confirmation.

"Good morning," Beatrice said as she went past the couch and into the kitchen.

"Morning," they said in unison.

"Thank you for texting me last night, Shane. I would've worried." She opened the baking cabinet and removed a metal mixing bowl. "I'm making pancakes. What do you guys want in them?"

"Do we have chocolate chips?" Noah asked.

"Yep. Shane, will you eat blueberries in yours?"

"Yes, please."

The clatter of breakfast preparations continued behind them.

"What do you boys want in your pancakes?" Beatrice said. "Hold on… I just asked you that. My mind sometimes."

Noah released a trembling breath after his grandmother's words. Shane put his arm around the kid's shoulders as they focused on the film.

•   •   •

Dread loomed over the crowd as the top half of the ninth ended. The Brigs trailed 5 to 2. Some fans packed it in early, while the loyal ones, or the more superstitious, hung around Hinton Fields even as the night dragged.

J.J. singled off a poorly aimed fastball when he went up to bat. Shane was on deck and it had been a lousy night for him offensively, with a strikeout and two fly-outs. The season would be over soon if he couldn't find a way to continue the rally. He checked the sidelines as his walkup music played and saw Noah was still on the basketball court, alternating between shooting hoops and watching the game.

Find a way to stay for him.

He tightened his gloves and eased into his stance, awaiting the first pitch from Taylor Maggio, the ace closer of the Nauset Admirals.

Maggio's leg left the mound like he was about to deliver the pitch, but instead he pivoted and launched the ball to his first baseman. J.J. tried to rush back, but he had already taken a lead toward second.

It was too late. The first-base umpire declared him out.

Shane came out of his stance. "That was a balk."

The officials conferred by home plate as Coach Hale came jogging onto the diamond. Shane backed away to let his coach handle the argument. Through the open windows of the press box, he could hear the P.A. announcer clarify the situation in the broadcast booth for viewers watching the livestream of the game.

"It's like an act of deception," he said. "Anytime the pitcher has already started the motions that indicate he is about to release the ball, from that point onwards, he has to see the pitch through. There's no readjusting, no attempts to pick baserunners. So the umpire saying J.J. is out is a questionable call if Maggio committed a balk."

Players on both teams grew restless and agitated as the review continued. What started as whispers in the crowd quickly became heckles. All the fans had two cents to throw in, especially with a ninth inning, down-for-the-count, about to decide the playoffs kind of call.

"Do you even play baseball?" Hale asked the first-base umpire.

"I don't play. I call games," the man answered.

"Yeah, we know you don't play," a belligerent Brigs fan shouted from the stands, his whole posse jeering behind him.

"You need to admit you made a bad call," Hale said.

"You want to get kicked out of here?" the umpire threatened.

Shane backpedaled to the same spot of fencing where Lexi held his hand the night before. His ears were turning red as he witnessed the veins in his coach's neck bulge.

Don't let him get ejected.

We need him here to win.

Please, God. I'm not ready to leave yet.

Then the lights cut. The crowd and the players were alarmed at the darkness for a moment before they realized it was harmless.

"Ain't this just the cherry on the sundae?" Hale said as he marched off to the Rec Center. "This conversation is not over."

Lexi poked her head out from the press box windows and addressed the crowd. "We're sorry, folks. We don't know the source of the power outage at this point or how long it will be before the lights are back."

Half of the remaining crowd filed out after the announcement. Shane eyed the basketball court and saw Noah was no longer there.

The Brigs in the dugout seemed uncertain of what to do with the extended delay.

"Huddle up," Shane commanded.

The team formed a large circle by the first baseline. Lucas took his place beside Shane and knocked on his captain's batting helmet. "Do you know you're still wearing this?"

"Thank you." His head felt lighter once he removed the gear.

"Will they give the win to the Admirals if we don't get the lights back?" Jermaine asked.

"They can't do that," said J.J.

"Sure they can," Matt replied. "We made it through more than five innings. They'll count that as a complete Cove League game."

"That won't happen," Shane said. "I know this might sound crazy, but I swear… Three seconds before the lights cut, I was praying for a sign."

"Good work, Shane," Dennis said. "This is a real shitty sign."

"It is not," Shane said. "We're getting a chance to clean the slate right now, to regroup. Can't you see that? The second those lights come back on, this is a brand new ballgame."

The guys glared back, most of them shooting him dubious looks.

"Anyone have gum?" Dennis asked.

Shane saw Lexi hovering a few feet away, waiting for the team meeting to end. "Let's hit pause for a minute."

Lexi tossed Shane his outdated flip phone once he walked over. "I found that in the press box," she said. "Do you think it's some sort of prehistoric technology?"

"Very funny. Is that all you came over here for?" Shane felt silly once he asked the question. He thought the kiss in the dream had been real for a moment and he was disappointed she was acting like nothing happened.

"I thought you could use a laugh," she said. "It feels tense out here."

"Tell me about it. I have to get some confidence in these guys before the blackout ends. Got any ideas?"

Her smartphone beeped and she checked the screen. "How's that for timing? Max just texted me. Should I ask him?"

"No. Don't tell him I'm stuck."

"Okay, chill." She put her phone away and peered up at the floodlights. "Why don't you do the prayer?"

"We do that *before* games."

"Alright. Why don't you sing a song?"

"A song… Lexi, you're a genius."

Shane hopped up the bleachers. There was still no sign of Noah in the basketball court and the snack shack had already closed for the night. Then he saw the boy leaving from the side doors of the Rec. "Noah, come here."

The boy stalled with a slow walk over. "What's going on?" he asked, frightful of Shane's urgent tone.

"I need you to sing for us."

"What? Why?"

"To rally the guys."

"But I've never sung in public." Noah said, mortified at the prospect.

"Wouldn't this be a cool debut? We need something to get us charged and I think it could be that song of yours."

"'Wildball?'"

"That's the one. I know if the guys hear it, it'll make them feel the same way I do."

"And how is that?"

Shane smiled. "Like I am where I'm supposed to be."

"I don't have a keyboard though."

"Just do it solo. That's how the people that sing 'The Star-

Spangled Banner' do it."

"'*Wildball'*s not exactly the national anthem."

"It isn't *yet*."

"There's not even a microphone."

"Please, Noah. I'm asking a lot, but it's only 'cause I know you can do it."

The boy rolled his eyes. "Fine," he said begrudgingly.

"Great." Shane hurried down the stands with Noah before the boy could change his mind. The huddle had disbanded, but the team still hung out together on the warning track.

"Listen up, Brigs." Shane tapped into the deepest register of his voice to get their attention. "This is my friend, Noah. He has something we need to hear."

The towering group of athletes waited with their arms folded.

Noah cleared his throat. "Do you remember the first line?" he asked Shane. "Wait. I remember." He began with his head down, his black hair shielding him from seeing the ballpark.

"Always fall asleep with the TV on
Your dreams get funded by..."

Noah's hands shook. He stopped singing once he saw the awkward glances from the baseball players. "I'm sor –"

"One, two, three, four." Shane clapped his hands to make quarter notes.

Noah was stunned as the shortstop restarted the song on his own.

"Always fall asleep with the TV on
Your dreams get funded by telethons
Coca Cola bottles for target practice
Gotta make it home for pancake breakfast"

Shane held his hands high to signal the guys to clap once Noah sang again. Lucas and Jermaine held down the beat. Then Roman and J.J. followed suit and a moment later the whole team was in sync.

"Give us a frown
Like we're saving a stray
Hope you did your stretches
For these big brother days"

The fans tuned into the performance as Noah sang from his gut.
"A ghost on your shoulder
A hero down the hall
Catch it if you can
The wildball
You're as tall as the floodlights
When the crowds all call
But don't spend your life chasing
A wildball"

Shane gestured for the guys to chime in. Some guessed at the unfamiliar words while others just hummed the melody.
"A ghost on your shoulder
A hero down the hall
Catch it if you can
The wildball
You're as tall as the floodlights"

The shine of the ballpark's lights returned right after they sang Noah's lyric. All the Brigs went wide-eyed from the synchronicity. They cheered like they had already won and hoisted Noah up on their shoulders like he had made the play that saved the game.

• • •

There was no chance of sleep after the victory. He replayed the night like a film in his head and waited until dawn to ride to Trunk Drive for an early morning swim. The only other soul on the beach was an old man fishing off the jetty.

Shane left his things by the lifeguard shack where he had been staying only a few weeks prior. The ocean slowed his thoughts and made him conscious of his aching muscles. When the skin on his fingers shriveled, he returned to the comfort of his towel.

He got his cell phone out of the drawstring bag he brought with him. He had charged the device after Lexi returned it but had yet to check his messages. An exchange of texts with Kev from Tuesday night sat at the top of the inbox.

I never got back to him.

There was a notification for three missed calls, all from Kev, late Tuesday night. Then he listened to a new voicemail from Jenny: "Shane. It's Mom. Call me back as soon as you get this. There's something I need to tell you."

The salt water that wet his hair and covered his back turned cold as he called his mother. He prayed he was wrong about the reason for her doleful tone as he waited for her to answer.

"Shane?" she said.

"Mom, I got your voicemail. What's wrong?"

"It's bad news. But I wanted to make sure you heard it from me."

"Did something happen?"

"You haven't heard yet?"

"Is it Kev?"

Jenny cleared her throat. "He's dead. I'm so sorry. I've been calling 'cause I didn't want it to be like Coach Calloway again, but your phone's been off."

His gut wrenched as a charcoal cloud consumed the sky. The beach fell out of focus. He shut his eyes and listened to the morning current until he could form a sentence. "When did it happen?"

"Yesterday at about three in the morning."

The missed calls.

He was trying to get a hold of you.

"What happened to him?"

"Kev was out in the streets late at night. He was lying down in the middle of the road. I don't know if he passed out, or if he had been drinking, but a police cruiser hit him. The officer was speeding because he had an emergency call. He must not have seen Kev until it was too late."

"Where was this?"

"It was close to where Coach Calloway's car accident was."

Shane listened to Jenny's sniffling.

"I can't imagine what his parents are going through right now," she said. "Shane... Shane, are you okay?"

He focused on the black.

Another nightmare. That's all this is.

He readied to lift his eyelids. He was going to wake up back at Beatrice's house. There would be no sea before him and his mother's voice would vanish from his ears. Kev would cheat the death Shane had cooked up for him in this terrible dream.

"Shane?" Jenny asked over the phone. "Are you there?"

Shane opened his eyes and saw the waves wash over the sand, leaving a trail of slick foam behind them. "Yeah, Mom. I'm here."

CHAPTER TWENTY-TWO

"Withdraw"

The night air was still cold in May, so Shane and Kev both wore their gray St. Francis sweatshirts as they walked the streets of Astors.

"What was it you wanted to talk about?" Kev asked.

"Not yet," Shane said. Calloway's house was the next on the block. The doors of the black truck were open in the driveway and it looked like there were bags of groceries filling the vehicle. "Let's cross."

They hurried to the other side of the street as the stained glass on Calloway's front door lit up like a red beacon. Shane glanced at the home before averting his eyes to the sidewalk, where his sneakers moved in tandem with Kev's canvas hi-tops.

"You never told me about that dinner you had with Coach." Kev nodded toward Calloway's house.

"It was weird," Shane replied.

"You must've said something to piss him off. Because I've started way more at shortstop ever since you went over there."

You should tell him the truth.

"I saw my first naked woman on this street," Kev said. "I was just riding my bike around when I saw her through an open window.

How about you? Where'd you see your first naked lady?"

"The internet."

Kev laughed then pointed to a nearby hilltop playground. "Let's go to Benefit Park. We can talk up there. Plus the stargazing is prime."

You can't tell him.

He might not believe you.

What if he tells Calloway about it?

"I actually don't feel well," Shane said. "I think I'm gonna walk home."

"We met up because *you* wanted to talk."

"I know but my stomach is off. Let's hang out this weekend."

Kev held onto Shane's shoulder to keep him from leaving. "What's going on with you, man?"

"I'm just stressed with finals coming up."

"It's not that. Your eyes looked like you died."

Shane stared down at the sidewalk. There were hopscotch squares drawn in chalk beneath his feet. The numbers led uphill towards the playground.

"I have to go. See you in school tomorrow." Shane crossed the street. He turned to call back to Kev, but his friend was already gone.

•　　　•　　　•

The neighborhood kids were out with the morning sun on Beatrice's block. Shane hopped off his bike and walked by a yard where a mother was chasing her giggling daughters with mist from the garden hose.

You could have saved him.

In the next driveway, a pack of middle school skateboarders practiced manuals.

Was his death instant?

He pictured Kev on a slab in the morgue. Blue and pale.

The cops will have his phone. They'll see he was calling me.

He saw Noah and another boy standing in the street, craning their necks as a toy drone descended from the sky.

It's gonna come out. Everything about Calloway is gonna come out.

Noah waved. "How was the water?"

"Nice," Shane said. "Can we raincheck on the bike ride? I didn't sleep well."

"Definitely. Aidan is showing me his new drone anyway."

The kid tinkered with the remote as it flew off the grass and hovered over Shane's head.

"It can be your angel, Shane." Noah joked.

"How are you shivering? It's summer," Aidan said.

Shane peered down at his hands and realized the boy was right. He caught a glimpse of his haggard reflection in the front windows of Beatrice's home. The dresser drawers were flung open and the couch cushions had been overturned. "What happened here?"

A basket of clean laundry was on the floor and his gray St. Francis hoodie sat at the top of it. The chill in his body subsided as he put another layer on. He thought of Kev and wondered if he was wearing their high school sweatshirt when he got hit.

Your eyes look like you died.

Shane went to the kitchen and filled a mason jar from the tap. Water spilled down his cheeks as he chugged. He noticed the oven's front burner was switched to its highest setting though there was nothing cooking on the range.

Purple post-it notes completely lined the cabinet doors. Some of the messages were written in red ink, others in a dying blue sharpie: light bulbs, dentist on Tuesday @ 315, call Louise, Shane return flight, call Louise back, Noah – school supplies.

The fridge door was decorated in the papers as well: Take garbage out THURSDAY. WHOLE MILK for NOAH.

"I don't understand where it went." Beatrice came in the kitchen wearing her shirt inside-out.

"What are you looking for?"

"I can't find Lyla's necklace anywhere. Noah will be devastated if it's gone. I'm sorry I went through your dresser but – "

"I have it." Shane took off the necklace and handed it over.

"Thank God." Beatrice held it close to her chest for a moment.

"Why have you been wearing it?"

"I … I'm not sure. I'm sorry. I should've asked."

"Yes. You should have asked Noah if it was okay," she chided him. "And I just wasted an hour looking for it. I turned the house upside-down. You could have spared me the trouble."

"I really am sorry." His fingers were drawn towards his sternum, which suddenly felt unarmed.

Beatrice examined the post-its on the cabinet doors, tossing some and allowing others to remain. "Shane, I need to know what day you're leaving. I'm trying to make some plans with family and we'll need the space here."

"I don't know if it's the best idea for me to leave."

"What do you mean?"

"Don't you think it would be good if we were both here to look out for Noah?"

"But you have to go back to school."

"It's just –" He switched the front burner off before he continued. "You've been forgetting things and it doesn't feel right to leave without… Maybe you should get that checked out by a doctor, before I go."

Beatrice clenched Lyla's necklace in her palm. "I welcomed you into this home when no one else would. I remember that much."

"I didn't mean to –"

"It's not your place; to look out for Noah or to tell me that I'm unfit to."

He exited without saying another word and rode his bike down the street. The neighbor's drone followed, but after a minute the buzzing faded.

●　　●　　●

Shane snatched the last of the plastic figures and raised it over his head so the flag brushed against his hair. He tripped on a tree root as he launched the green dude into Stag's Pond. The fading red lights were waiting for him in the night sky when he landed on his back.

"You want them to be haunted," he said.

Then from behind came the sound of branches cracking. He shot up from the dirt and saw a shadow emerging from the brush.

It can't be...

He squinted and tried to make out the features. "Who's there?"

"Shane? That you?" someone asked in a Southern accent.

"Lucas. I thought you were..."

"Thought I was who?"

"I don't know... A ghost."

"What happened to the green dudes?" Lucas pointed to the collection of buoyant figures in the pond.

"I killed them," Shane admitted.

"You do have a touch for theatrics."

"How'd you know to find me here?"

"Noah and Beatrice were worried about you. They said you'd been gone all day and weren't answering your phone. So they got in touch with Coach Hale and then he got in touch with me. And I knew where you'd be." Lucas sat on the ground and swatted at mosquitoes. "You want to tell me what's going on?"

"I've been wearing the cross necklace. The one Noah left when I found him here." Shane motioned at the pond. "It was in Beatrice's guest room where I stay. And she was panicking earlier because she couldn't find it."

"You hadn't told her you'd been wearing it?"

"No. And I don't... Maybe I wanted to feel closer to something. But when I had to give the necklace back today, it was like the jig was up." Shane tossed a rock in the water and watched the ripples vanish. "You'll laugh at this. I even thought that power outage during the Admirals game...I thought it was..."

"You thought it was God?"

"A spirit. God. Something."

"Who's to say it wasn't?" Lucas saw tears stream down his friend's cheeks. "Shane, did something bad happen?"

"Last night... my friend Kev was out in the middle of the road back in Oregon. He was drunk maybe, or maybe he just passed out,"

Shane said as his breathing became fragmented. "There was a cop that was responding to an emergency call and he didn't see Kev. He got hit and how he's dead."

"I'm so sorry," Lucas said.

"Before it happened, Kev was trying to get a hold of me, but I was asleep in the press box."

"Why was Kev calling you?"

"'Cause we both..." Shane dropped his head and spoke towards the dirt: "We were both abused by the same coach back at St. Francis."

Lucas hugged Shane. "How long have you been carrying that around?"

"Too long."

"Am I the first person you've told?"

"Besides Kev, yeah."

"So he was calling you to talk about the coach?"

"Calloway was his name. He targeted Kev once I went to college. I don't know how bad it got. Kev wanted to come clean about it all. Tell people who Calloway really was. And I didn't. I told Kev to stop calling me about it. So he had no one to talk to about all the messed up shit in his head, and if I could've just answered my fucking phone."

Shane backed away from the edge of the water and into the trees. He crouched down and covered his head with his arms.

"Hey, you can't put that on yourself." Lucas pushed off the ground. He went over to Shane and rubbed his back as the sobs became hysterical.

"But I didn't help him," Shane said.

"You didn't kill him either."

"It feels like I did."

"You aren't the one that needs to be forgiven."

"What about Kev's family? If I told them everything I just told you, do you think they'd say I was off the hook? I could have helped him and instead I told him to get lost."

"That's quite a burden to go around carrying your whole life. And it's not yours to bear."

Shane fell over and let his body hit the dirt. "I'm not going back to Oregon. I want to stay here and look out for Noah."

"Don't make that decision tonight." Lucas offered a hand to help Shane up, but he refused to rise.

"The kid's mom is dead. His Dad took off. His grandmother's starting to lose it."

"So how are you next in line?"

"You're the one that believes in God. Think about the way it all worked out this summer. When I came here that night and found him... Maybe I'm the one that's supposed to take care of him."

"You have to take care of yourself first, man." Lucas sat by Shane as he wriggled in the brush. "You need to establish yourself."

"So I just abandon Noah?"

"What are you gonna do if you stay here? Work at the sporting goods store? Coach little league?"

"I'd find a job."

"What about baseball?"

"I could transfer to a school in Boston eventually."

"It sounds like you've thought this through."

"Fuck off, Lucas."

"I won't. I don't have a team I get to go back to next week. This is where it ends for me. So I'm sorry but you don't get to quit."

"I can't do this." Shane lifted himself up and returned to the water.

"You have to think long-term," Lucas said. "Not just for you, but for Noah, too. If you're that invested in helping this kid, how are you going to be more of an asset to him? Or to your family?"

Shane was too exhausted to stay stubborn against the truth. "By finishing." He regained focus in his eyes and eased out of his erratic breathing.

"That's right."

"By making it to the next level." Shane used his sleeve to wipe the snot from his face.

"Baseball is what you were born to do. You have to go back to Oregon."

"But what's gonna happen to Noah?"

"He'll be okay. You have to trust in that. He did have a pretty great role model this summer."

A steady buzz came from his cell phone. Shane took it out of his sweatshirt pocket and saw an unfamiliar number on the screen.

"Who is it?" Lucas asked.

"Area code is Oregon. It could be the cops..."

"Calling about Kev?"

"Probably. What do I do?" Shane turned back and saw Lucas leaning against a tree trunk.

"Just be honest."

Shane accepted the call and placed the phone against his cheek. "Hello?"

CHAPTER TWENTY-THREE

"Til the Ninth"

Picture Lake was tucked away between secret paths and cranberry bogs. It was a muggy morning, so Shane and Noah went to the lake to cool off.

"Do you think you'll come back next summer?" Noah asked, gripping onto a rope swing.

Shane sat on a stump by the edge of the lake. He was tired of jumping in the water and also a little fearful of the nearby swans. He used a tree branch to push rocks and pebbles around in the dirt, tending to his own Zen garden. "I don't know. We'll see how things go tonight."

The Brigs won the first matchup of the series against Waterford the day before, so even if they lost the next one there would be another shot at the championship title in a potential third game.

"If you win..." Noah paused. The waterproof cover that protected his cast made holding the rope difficult, but after some adjustments he was able to launch into a cannonball. "I'll never see you again."

"That's not true," Shane called out as Noah swam through the ripples of his splash. "I might come back and visit. Or maybe you'll come to Oregon. We'll cross paths again."

Noah came out of the water and eyed the branch in Shane's hand. "Can I see that?"

Shane tossed it over and watched the boy admire its smoothness.

"This is perfect for carving something. Do you care if I keep it?"

"All yours," Shane said. "Did you hear what I was saying though?"

A solemn mood came over the boy as he nestled the branch. "I actually have something to tell you…

"What's up?"

Noah grabbed his towel off a large rock and dried his hair. He let the cloth cover his face as a way to hide. "I made it so the lights cut that night you beat Nauset."

"What? How did you even…?" A slideshow played backwards in his mind of the game when the floodlights went out. He remembered his teammates carrying Noah, the boy singing his song, and the argument between Hale and the umpires. "I don't understand."

Noah poked his head out from under his towel. "Lucas showed me how to kill the lights last summer."

"Why would he do that?"

"We were bored one day at workshops. It's super random, but the controls are actually somewhere in Maine."

"I know," Shane said. "You have to call an office to switch the lights off. How did you know the number?"

"It's written on the base of one of the lights," the boy explained. "I borrowed a friend's cell phone and I called the people in Maine and told them the game had ended early."

"Why would you do that?"

"It seemed like you guys were going to lose. I thought it might give you a chance to win. And it worked." Noah gave a nervous smile, thinking he could trick Shane into thanking him.

"But it's like the Brigs made it to the championship based on a lie now."

"I don't get why you're so mad."

"'Cause you made it an unfair fight."

"So you aren't happy you won?"

"It's not about winning. It's about you lying."

"I just..." Noah bit his lip as he tried to form his thoughts. "I knew if you guys lost that night..."

"What?"

The boy stared at a family approaching the lake. The mother pushed twins in a double stroller while the father held on to a pair of accelerating German Shepherds. "Forget it." Noah chucked the branch into the dirt and stormed off.

After the family passed, Shane picked up the smooth stick from the ground. He went up the rocky slope to the path where he and Noah had left their bikes and belongings. Noah had already buckled up his helmet and slipped on his shoes, ready to speed away.

"Hold up."

"What?" the boy snapped.

"It's a hard thing to tell the truth. I wish I were better at it." Shane handed the branch to Noah. "I'm proud of you."

"You're not mad?"

"You learned from the mistake, right?"

"Yeah," Noah mumbled.

"Then I'm not mad."

•　　　•　　　•

The sun had set by the time he arrived at the Rec. Noah left his bike next to Shane's in the rack and walked around back to Hinton Fields. He felt like he was at school assembly or the summer fair as he moved through the mass of people. Kids from workshop directed head nods his way. Tourists checked out the Brigs swag at the merchandise table. Old men that smelled like cigars and aftershave mingled at the top of Spectator's Hill. Noah stopped near them to examine the diamond and saw Shane take the plate under a silver sky.

The boy removed a five-dollar bill from his pocket as he followed the warm smell of the snack shack. He fantasized about sprinkling powdered sugar and cinnamon onto a piece of fried dough. His stomach took the driver's seat as he forgot his original mission. He rushed through the ballpark until he saw Lucas leaning against the protective fencing along the first base line. Noah patted him on the back and stuck his good hand out for a fist pound. "What's up, Lucas?"

"Hey, Noah," Lucas said. "How's much longer with the cast?"

"Not sure. It's on the mend though. How's your bat tonight?"

"Just struck out. Looks like Shane's planning on doing the same."

Noah was distracted by a wave of fog rolling off the harbor and onto the field. The floodlights kicked on and Noah zoned in on the bits of mist he could see cavorting under the brightness. "Score tied?"

"Since the second. And now here we are in the fifth. Pitchers have been quality and the bats haven't warmed up yet. To be completely honest, it's dragging. I can smell the extra innings."

"I can't stick around. I just wanted to get this to Shane." Noah pulled a sealed envelope out of his shorts pocket and handed it over to Lucas.

"Don't you guys live together?"

"Yeah, but I – I just wanted him to have it tonight."

"He's about to –"

"I can't stay though," Noah insisted. "Will you just make sure he gets it?"

Lucas drew a pretend X over his heart with his index finger then placed the letter in his pants pocket.

"Thanks." Noah backed away from the fence. "What do you think? Should I buy fried dough before I go or will it make me sick when I'm biking home?"

"I think you just answered your own question."

They waved goodbye to each other as Noah navigated his way up the hill through the families that eagerly watched the game unfold.

• • •

Shane sprung up from the grass and snatched the line drive. He pivoted mid-air to face second base and hurled the ball to Matt for the double play.

The acrobatics ended the top of the ninth and earned Shane a round of applause. It was still a tie game and the crowd's mood was shifting between boredom and anxiety. Shane hated how stalemates dulled the fans. Once things got stagnant, baseball became a test of patience instead of a fun pastime.

Fog covered the field. It traveled in sheets over the players as they returned to the dugouts. But Shane saw a different kind of fog hovering by the press box, a darker and murkier one.

"Is that smoke?" Jermaine asked as he lifted his catcher's mask and peered at the structure.

Shane ran behind the building as word of the fire spread throughout Hinton Fields and the game was put on hold. Shane held the door for the distressed crew of interns rushing out of the structure.

"What happened?" Shane asked.

"We had too much stuff plugged in," one of the teens said. "The outlet started sizzling."

Lexi was the last to come downstairs. She had a strange look on her face once she saw Shane waiting outside.

"You okay?" he asked.

"Yeah. It's just... It'll sound stupid," she said.

"Tell me."

"I had a dream the other night where you went running into a burning building."

"I had a dream where you told me something about fire," he said, breathless.

They locked eyes for a moment, unsure what to make of the subconscious overlap, then they both watched the smoke as it thickened.

Sirens drew near and Shane knew he didn't have much time. "I have to go up there," he said.

"Why?" Lexi asked.

"I don't know. I just do."

He went up the stairs two at a time and felt a change in air once he was halfway up. As he made it to the top, he started coughing and questioned his decision. The flame grew by windows that overlooked the ballpark. It was almost like there was a burning picture frame forming around the diamond.

What Lexi said in my dream: Fire on the diamond. That's when he'll come.

The umpires opened the back fence for the arrival of the fire truck, which raced down the track and parked by the press box.

Shane retreated and stepped aside as the firefighters stormed in. The truck's red flashers left him feeling fuzzy and disoriented as he came back down. Players and fans craned their necks, trying to watch the first responders extinguish the fire through the press box windows, but Shane backed away from the chaos. He saw Lucas was sitting alone in the dugout and he made his way over.

"That smoke get in your head, Shane?" Lucas said.

Shane sat beside his friend. "Something's off. Can you feel it?"

"There are some vibes flying around. Or it's that 'til the ninth feeling."

"What's that?"

"It's something my Dad says: 'Don't wait 'til the ninth to decide you want to win.'"

"Hey, you're up to bat next," Shane said. "You ending this thing for us?"

"Shane, this might be the last real game I ever compete in. That ball's about to skyrocket all the way to our weird, secret pond."

"Damn straight."

"Shit. I just remembered. Noah wanted me to give you something. I forgot where I put it."

"Give it to me after we win. Okay?"

The coaches received permission to continue the game while the firefighters examined the structure. The players resumed their positions for the bottom of the ninth.

"Sorry about the delay there, folks." The intern who did P.A. announcements had wrangled up a megaphone and spoke to the crowd in a distorted voice from the sidelines. "We'll now resume the game with Lucas Barnes up to bat for the Brigs."

Once play resumed, the Waterford Breakers brought out their star pitcher, Andy Bergan. Lucas cracked a line drive off the first pitch he threw. The ball bounced around in the corner of left field, making the outfielders scramble. By the time the defense got organized, Lucas had made it all the way to third base.

Shane waited on deck. He would aim for the gaps in the outfield and hopefully buy Lucas enough time to make the game-winning run.

"And now up to bat for the Brigs is Shortstop Shane Monoghan," the intern announced from the megaphone.

No walkup music followed his introduction. Shane eyed Lexi like somehow she could help him through the unnerving silence.

Hale motioned his player forward, eager for him to capitalize on Lucas' momentum.

Fog swarmed Hinton Fields and with the red flashers of the fire truck, the cloud over the ballpark was illuminated by a mechanical shade of red. The same monster Shane saw on the night of his arrival had caught up to him at last.

Calloway.

He tried to focus on Bergan but forgot to swing at the first pitch; a fastball aimed low. It cut the outside corner of the strike zone. 0-1 count.

Then a pit formed in his stomach. Shane put his bat down for a moment and placed his hands around his neck, like he needed to remove someone's grip from it.

Thought you could outrun me?

He lifted his bat and stared at the pitcher in the middle of the red smoke. Instead of the young man named Bergan, it was Calloway's face that stared back from the mound.

Shane wasn't locked in anymore. He got duped by a changeup and earned a second strike. The crowd sighed with disappointment.

His thoughts began to spiral. He had a flash of Noah's bleeding hand and heard his hysterical shrieks. He remembered puking into Stag's Pond and Calloway's hand creeping up his thigh.

Shane withheld at a pitch that went way outside the strike zone. 1-2 count.

Get a grip.

He looked back to the pitcher's mound and saw the twenty-something kid from California instead of the phantom that was there moments before.

Shane stalled with an at-bat ritual so he could collect himself. First, he crunched his shoes against the gravel, then rotated his shoulder cuffs a few times before assuming his usual stance.

The pitcher and catcher finished their unspoken negotiations. Shane exhaled.

He swung at the low ball and heard it make contact with a pop against the wood. Shane ran. What he hoped would be a missile into right field was thwarted when the pitcher stuck his glove out.

Shane eased up, thinking he was about to be out, but the pitcher flubbed the catch. The ball had ricocheted off his mitt and was on a new trajectory. Shane sprinted again as the pitcher fell to the dirt.

Since there was no runner on second base, Lucas could remain safe at third and not risk getting tagged out. But as the ball made its way to the clutches of the infielders, Lucas decided to charge home.

What is he doing?

The Waterford shortstop and third baseman both jockeyed for the ball as it bounced around frenetically.

Shane faced forward again and continued on his path. His neck's quick motion caused his batting helmet to fly off his head. He was almost at first base, but he was too baffled by what Lucas had done and too hungry for the outcome to keep looking straight ahead. He performed one more quick check, turning to his left as he continued his dead bolt.

Lucas slid into home right as the recovered ball was thrown to the catcher.

"Hey!"

Shane was inches away from the first baseman. It was too late to stop the crash. He had made a rookie baserunning mistake. He was staring at the scenery and ended up driving into the wrong lane of traffic. The two young men collided and a flash of white consumed Shane's vision.

Then it was daytime. He heard the wail of a detuning orchestra, though the ballpark was empty except for him and Gus-the-batboy.

Gus stood at the far end of the Rec and went toward the Dip Corner. Shane jogged over, trying to stop the kid from learning of his heroes' bad habits. As Shane got closer to the batboy, he saw him tear a loose thread from his jersey. Gus yanked at the string until it was several feet long then skipped around the back of the building. The black cotton guided him like markers on a path.

Shane made it to the Dip Corner and found Lexi waiting there. She walked backwards with her microphone in hand. Its thin cable continued the trail he was to follow. He wanted to ask Lexi where it would take him, but she darted into an alcove.

The cable led him down a dark, cold hallway. Shane struggled to keep his footing as the ground turned to ice. He panicked as he realized he had dropped the cord, but then he saw a room emitting a red glow at the end of the corridor.

The space was dank and bare. A heat lamp swung from the rafters, and in the center of the room, a man performed chin-ups between two sets of lockers. The man had his back turned to Shane, but somehow he knew that it was Calloway.

Shane inched closer as his former coach kept exercising. "You're still so angry," Calloway said.

The booming voice made Shane jump back.

"I can see it coming off you," Calloway said. "Like heat on the pavement."

Shane tried to speak though his lips made no movements, like muscles withered from atrophy.

"Know this," Calloway said. "Whatever I did, I did it to make you feel like a man."

All you ever

His lips were still stuck. Shane massaged his throat and pried his mouth open. He vocalized at first until he was able to find words again. "All you ever made me feel like was a bug you were trying to squash." Shane moved around the space so he could face the phantom.

"Oh, nut up." Calloway remained focused on his chin-ups.

"How can you still do so many? Aren't you dead?"

"As dead as you let me be." Calloway dropped to the floor and signaled his student to take over.

Shane glanced up at the metal bar then heard an impatient grunt from Calloway.

"Who was it that broke you?" Shane asked, placing his hand on Calloway's shoulder before it got smacked away.

"You want to end up like him?" Calloway opened one of the lockers. The door gave way to a pocket of the cosmos. Kev was suspended in the air horizontally in the middle of the black sky. His body was paralyzed. His eyes were vacant, frozen.

"How do the stars look tonight, Kev?" Calloway snickered. "Ah, he can't hear me."

Shane tried to go through the locker to wake his friend before Calloway closed the door. "You don't want to do that."

Shane opened the locker a second time but there was just a compartment in it, with mounted hooks for hanging clothes. He closed the door and let his hand rest on the metal, longing for contact that never came.

"How many chin-ups can you do these days?" Calloway asked.

"I don't have time for you anymore." Shane saw a fierce light appear inside the locker. He opened it and saw a way back to Hinton Fields.

"Go tell the world how terrible I was," Calloway dared him. "See how much it changes."

"I'm not afraid to speak ill of the dead." Shane stepped inside the locker.

"What about Noah? Something bad will happen." Calloway hopped up to the bar, resuming his endless endeavor. "And you won't be here to save him."

"He won't need me to."

• • •

Shane had the locker room to himself since the other guys were either still celebrating somewhere or fast asleep in their beds. The shower's hot water coursed down his back as he closed his eyes. When Lucas slid home and was declared safe a few hours prior, the Brigs charged the diamond and formed a victory pile on top of the leftfielder. But the glory was cut short by the Breakers' first baseman alerting the coaches that Shane was unresponsive on the ground.

The firefighters that were still on the field transported Shane to the hospital where he underwent an MRI. The test made him feel like he was trapped in some kind of experimental, compact nightclub, as a half hour of bizarre percussion and malfunctioning strobe lights overloaded his brain. At the end of it, the doctors diagnosed Shane with his first concussion.

Since he could walk without assistance, hold conversations, and had no feelings of dizziness or nausea, Shane was released to the care of Coach Hale. They drove to the Rec Center, where Shane said Beatrice would be along shortly to pick him up. It felt wrong to lie, but he wanted to be alone so he could decompress. Shane entered the facility through the back doors that Frank always left unlocked.

He was surprised to see an envelope waiting for him in his locker when he came out of the shower. He used the white towel around his waist to dry his fingers off then opened the seal. There was a folded sheet of notebook paper inside with big, blue-highlighter handwriting on it. He took a seat on the bench and read.

Shane,

I hope you can forgive me for cutting the lights. It was a dumb thing to do and I only did it because I wanted you to stay for another week. I get it now that I shouldn't have interfered with the game.

I'm really glad I got to know you this summer. Beatrice is too. Sometimes she does forget things but if it gets bad I will let someone know.

I thought that took guts when you told me you were proud of me today. In school, the teachers always say how it takes courage to stand up to bullies.

For me, it's a lot harder to just be honest with the people I love. So I wanted to write you this letter 'cause it's easier for me to write things than it is for me to say them.

I think what you're doing is awesome and I want to be like you someday. The amount of work you put into your sport is amazing. I know you're going to make it to the Majors. I hope you'll remember me when you're a star.

Sincerely,
Noah

He read the letter two more times before he stood up and got dressed. Then some buried feeling overcame him when he went to tie his sneaker laces. His head fell into his hands as he let himself weep.

CHAPTER TWENTY-FOUR

"Departures"

The crowd cheered when Shane took the stage. With players, host families, coaches, and interns, there were about a hundred people in the hotel conference room where the Brigs Banquet was held.

Shane walked to the podium and set a folder down on the surface with a printed copy of his speech inside. He tapped the microphone once, then began, "Our time here is ending. And I'm going to miss my brothers." He stopped to try to lock eyes with his teammates, but the spotlights made it difficult to put faces into focus.

"On top of that, my actual brother Troy is returning to Iraq for his second deployment. Troy visited Burnsdale a few weeks ago and I didn't get the chance to introduce many of you to him. Now I'm starting to see there's not much difference between concealing pride and admitting shame. So I wanted to take this moment to acknowledge my brother Troy. I will miss him, too."

His nerves subsided with the first batch of clapping. Shane found his place on the page again.

"Earlier in the summer our teammate Max got called up to the Majors. The funny thing is he was sad when he told me the news.

There was this storm and we were holed up together in the dugout at Hinton Fields. I couldn't figure out why he was so upset that day. But now I think I get it. He had to leave this place behind, sooner than we had to.

"This summer was a way to keep baseball pure for just a little while longer. If only I knew that while it was happening. I wish I could appreciate things before they came to pass."

He wiped the perspiration off his forehead and felt a little dizzy as he saw Calloway's name printed in the next paragraph.

"In June, I found out Mike Calloway, my former high school coach, had died. It was a confusing kind of grief and it made me isolate from the team."

He went to turn to the next page and was surprised to see Noah's letter mixed into his folder. Shane saw the sloppily written words in blue highlighter and read a few of them; *it's a lot harder to just be honest with the people I love.* Then he flipped the letter over and saw the next page of his planned remarks waiting for him.

"I was going to talk a little about…"

He picked up Noah's letter, folded it, and placed it in his inside jacket pocket.

Just be honest.

He pushed aside his folder and adjusted the microphone. "Calloway was a bad coach. Sometimes I think he was punishing me for being talented. Whatever his reasons were, he was determined to rob me of something. I'm sad to say I let him do that. He… He was abusive."

Shane spoke over the piling whispers in the room, "He would berate me. Bully me. I was afraid whenever I heard him say my name. One night my senior year, he even tried to take advantage of me."

A palpable shock swept the space. The board members and host parents turned to Hale as if the patriarch should yank Shane off the stage. Hale waved for Shane to continue even though his player couldn't see the gesture.

"So I don't mourn for Calloway. I just wish I were brave enough to have said something when it would have mattered. Maybe…" He pulled back from the microphone. "Maybe I could have saved... But I..."

Shane grabbed at his stomach and winced. He looked down at the uncomfortable dress shoes on his feet for a minute before he felt someone tap him on the shoulder. It was Lucas, though it took Shane a moment to recognize him with his golden hair cut short.

"You want me to take over?" Lucas asked.

"No. I got it." Shane took a deep breath. "I should finish."

Lucas nodded and left the stage. Shane peered up, the lights too bright to tell if the crowd was even still there.

"A big part of the Cove League is our youth workshops where players get a chance to interact with kids in the community. Over the last eight weeks, I became friends with one of those kids.

"It's scary to know when someone is looking up to you. I guess it's because you're afraid they'll find out you aren't worthy of that admiration. And that's why I had to tell you all what I did. Whatever shine I still have through that kid's eyes, it wouldn't mean a thing if I were to stand up here and not be honest about what I've gone through. I hope you won't think less of me for it."

Shane stepped away from the podium and toward the red glow of the exit sign. He brushed past Lucas and went out the backdoor as delayed applause came from behind.

• • •

Noah shoved bundled socks into the duffle bag. The boy pulled his flat-rimmed Brigs cap over his face when Shane entered his bedroom.

"I was just doing the same thing." Shane pointed to the open bag on the floor. "You packing for Cooperstown?"

"Yep."

"You know you'll have a blast out there."

"Hope so." Noah placed a small, battery-powered keyboard in his luggage, along with a pair of electric blue headphones.

"You going to play 'Wildball' for the other kids?" Shane asked.

"Sometimes we sing on the bus."

"Well, I'm getting picked up real early tomorrow so I wanted to say goodbye tonight."

Shane waited for a hug, but Noah fidgeted with the zippers on his bag and kept his back turned.

"Have a safe flight," the boy said.

"Right. Thanks... Guess I'll see you later."

Shane went to leave the room, but he stopped short in the doorway. "Hey... I'm gonna miss you. Could I have a hug?"

Noah pulled his hat down over his face to hide his tears.

"Hey, it's okay," Shane said, as he also began to cry.

Noah looked up, revealing his bloodshot eyes and puffy cheeks. Shane went over and embraced him.

"I don't want you to go," Noah said.

"I wish I didn't have to."

Noah threw his hat off and let his head fall onto Shane's chest. They stayed that way for a while, safe in their pain.

"I love you," Shane said. "Look out for yourself, okay?"

"Okay." Noah backed away and placed his Brigs cap on again.

CHAPTER TWENTY-FIVE

"The Inferno"

Dear Shane,

I picked this postcard for you because of the deer on the front. (Sorry there were none with little-green-dudes.) I researched and found out the stag appears in someone's path when the veil between two worlds is thinnest. Make of that what you will. I've been applying for sportscaster jobs and I have an interview in Seattle for ESPN next month. Can we link up while I'm out West? Unless you're too famous now.

Love,
Lexi

P.S.
Did you hear Lucas got invited to play in a league in Japan?

P. P.S.
Text me Troy's address. We want to send him a care package.

• • •

Shane left the campus library and walked slowly through the hot September air, his body aching from the strength conditioning session and long night of paper writing. He peered into the windows of the campus pub and saw the upperclassmen throwing darts and nursing beers. Two young women stepped outside for a cigarette and did a double take of Shane.

"Is that him?" one of the girls asked.

"Shut up," her friend said.

Shane held tight onto the straps of his backpack as he passed. These encounters were becoming routine with the minor celebrity status he had gained on campus. Lexi's profile of the Monoghan Brothers was widely read after the video of Shane's confession went viral. There were articles about him on baseball sites and sports radio shows commented on the story for days. Some of his fellow students had approached him in the dining hall to tell him what he did was brave, while others gave him dirty looks on his way to morning lectures.

He returned to his single room. It was in a brownstone-style dorm across the hall from two astrophysics majors named Leanna and Jill. Shane went by their open door and saw the girls were watching television from their beds. A rocket ship exploded on the screen in a failed takeoff attempt.

"Whoa." Shane hovered in the doorway. "What happened?"

"That was a supply jet," Leanna said. "It was supposed to bring food to the astronauts on the space station."

"No one was on board," Jill clarified.

The three students observed the inferno unfold on the television.

"Shane, some of your mail came to our box again." Leanna pointed at a package on her nightstand.

"I haven't gotten any mail all semester, now I get two things in one day." He came into the room and grabbed the parcel.

Shane turned to leave but paused in the doorway again. "Well, I hope they have enough to eat in space 'til the next one comes."

"That *was* the next one," Leanna said.

A disheveled bed and mountain of dirty clothes waited for him across the hall. Baseball gear was spread out across the room and his desk was covered with articles for his Psychology classes.

He checked the package that had come for him and saw the return address was Beatrice's house in Burnsdale. There was no card or letter inside, only a necklace. Shane pulled out the beaded metal chain and admired the small, wooden crucifix attached to it. It wasn't the same one Noah wore, but a new one that had been hand-carved. His fingers recognized the feel of the wood.

The stick from Picture Lake. He made a cross from it.

Shane wanted to call Beatrice's landline to thank Noah, but it was late on the East Coast with the time difference.

He didn't want to lose the necklace, so he pulled out a shoebox from under his bed. There was a pile of concert tickets, family photos, and articles from the college paper about GSU baseball victories from last season. He knew it was odd to have so many personal artifacts tucked away but for the walls of his room to be free of decoration. Leanna and Jill kept nagging him about when he was going to move in.

In his box, he found the copy of the Nailer's Cove Times from the morning after the championship, along with the letter Noah wrote to him. It hurt to think back on the summer in Burnsdale. But it was the kind of hurt he wanted to keep close. He took off his GSU cap and tucked the cross under his shirt.

He set up his laptop at his desk, plugged his headphones in, and hit play on the whole Kings of Leon discography. Finishing the paper on time was going to require as much musical motivation as possible.

He noticed he forgot a heading, so he typed in the date.

September 21

Kev's birthday.

The whole day had gone by with Shane forgetting to pay any kind of tribute to his late friend.

Text his parents tomorrow.

He opened up the word document for his assignment. It was full of sentence fragments and verbal vomit. The thought of trying to turn it all into a coherent piece seemed too difficult, so he dropped his head.

Shane fell into a state of half-sleep and envisioned a snake coiling itself around his neck. When he came to, he flung himself off the desk as he felt something tying itself around him. No reptiles slithered away, just the headphones that had gotten tangled when he drifted off.

The intricate guitar of "Pyro" was still playing from the computer. Shane checked his phone and saw he had four unread texts from the college's emergency alert service. The first read: BARNETT COUNTY ON EVACUATION NOTICE FOR WILDFIRE.

There was a knock on his door before he could open the rest of the messages. "Shane," someone said. "Wake up."

He moved over to the door and opened it. "What's going on?"

Leanna and Jill stood before him in the hallway. "Forest fire," they said in unison.

"It's coming for us?"

"We're evacuating on buses," Jill said. "We need to get to King's."

It was the shorthand for the ivy-covered, upperclassmen dorm called King's Court.

"Are you coming?" The girls asked as they rushed out of the brownstone.

"I'll be right behind you guys," Shane shouted.

He grabbed his backpack and scrambled around his room, throwing his laptop, baseball glove, wallet, phone, keys, deodorant, toothbrush, socks and underwear inside. He'd be prepared if he ended up sleeping at a high school gymnasium three towns away. Right as he was about to leave, he stopped to make sure that Lexi's postcard was still in his pocket and that Noah's gift was around his neck.

Shane raced to King's with the sounds of sirens following and whirring helicopters overhead. He cleared the top of the hill and saw thousands of students in the quad. RA's shouted through megaphones for everyone to form single file lines as they waited for the buses to come.

Shane wandered past alarmed groups of freshman, one student in particular looking as though he was about to drop from a panic attack. He locked eyes with the boy and saw a genuine fear of death consuming him. The kid reminded him of Kev, with the same long, brown bangs slanting across his forehead.

You still haven't paid for what happened to him.

Students checked their phones for updates on the fire and looked around in distress. The collective anxiety seeped in and Shane's heart started to pound.

It's coming for you.

His chest kept tightening. He needed to get away from the crowd.

Shane pushed through the mob's outskirts and went for the trees at the edge of campus. Someone shouted his name, so he turned back for a moment. There was no way to tell who called for him in the bedlam. All he could see was dark silhouettes against the burning skyline.

Stop running from it already.

He heard his name again but gave up and faced the forest. Fearful voices continued to clamor in the background, though Shane felt calmer once he was alone in the woods. He focused on the patches of dead grass and the branches of the ash trees. As he walked along, he saw a figure near the trunks of the cedars, but he couldn't recognize the creature's strange shape.

Then it presented itself; a massive stag. With its sprawling antlers, it was as tall as a grown man. The stag bent his neck towards the ground and examined the grass. Shane took in its wonder, knowing the animal might flee once it saw him.

The stag paused when he spotted Shane. They held eye contact and Shane saw a stillness in the animal's gaze he had never felt from looking at a person.

He dropped into a crouched position, removed his backpack, and sat on the ground. After hesitating a moment, the stag continued browsing. Shane studied the night sky through the branches and noticed an orange glow was tainting the darkness. With the beast still aside him, he eased back, the air becoming hot and heavy.

Shane closed his eyes then felt something press against his foot.

He lifted his neck up and saw the stag had come closer. The animal bowed his head and nudged at Shane's feet, like it was telling him to leave.

Shane rose and threw his backpack over his shoulders. He stared into the creature's eyes, wishing he could save it. But the faint roaring of engines called for him alone. Shane ran out of the woods, leaving the beast behind him as the flames closed in.

View other Black Rose Writing titles at www.blackrosewriting.com/books and use promo code **PRINT** to receive a **20% discount** when purchasing.

BLACK ROSE
writing™